PRAYER
FOR THE
DYING

an enthralling Irish murder mystery

PETE BRASSETT

THE
BOOK
FOLKS

Paperback published by The Book Folks

London, 2018

ISBN 978-1-7181-5933-4

www.thebookfolks.com

Dedicated to
Thistle McTavish

Faithful friend and beloved companion.

2008 – 2018

*"You think dogs will not be in heaven?
I tell you, they will be there
long before any of us."*

Robert Louis Stevenson

Chapter 1

On no account was she to be disturbed. Nine hours. It was the absolute minimum required to ensure the day went without a hitch. Nine hours of uninterrupted slumber in a darkened room.

Maguire rolled gently from the bed, landed silently on all fours and crept stealthily towards the hall, his phone vibrating violently in his underpants. Grimacing, he closed the bathroom door, retrieved the handset and slumped against the bathtub.

'What feckin' time do you call this?' he said in a loud whisper, 'Do you want to wake the Beelzebub?'

O'Brien sniggered down the phone.

'Sorry, sir,' he said, 'but we've a religious relic that needs looking at. I think you ought to come.'

'A religious relic? Are you feckin' joking me?' hissed Maguire.

'This one, you've got to see,' said O'Brien.

'Right so,' sighed Maguire, 'where are you?'

'Saint Jerome's, in the field round the back.'

Fearful of rousing Mrs Maguire, he dressed as quickly, and as quietly as possible, watching her undulating form rise and fall with each wheezing breath.

'Like a lorry load of soda farls in a feckin' mail sack,' he muttered.

* * *

It was a little after six in the morning. The mist was lifting as Maguire, collar turned against the biting cold, crunched his way across the frost-bitten field towards O'Brien. They stood side by side and quietly contemplated the frozen, black mound that lay before them.

'What do you call a priest in a vegetable plot?'

'Dead.'

'Not much of a punch line, is it?' said Maguire. 'Who was he, Saint feckin' Fiachra?'

'Saint who?'

'Never mind. How long's he been here?'

'A while, I'd say. He's stiff as a frozen fish finger,' said O'Brien.

'Who found him?'

'One of the lads, sir, sixth former. Garda's taking a statement now.'

Maguire cupped his hands and blew on them, hard.

'Forensics?'

'Almost done, waiting on you before they carry him off.'

'Grand. Go on then,' he said, 'do the honours.'

O'Brien reluctantly knelt beside the cadaver, grabbed it with both hands and flipped it over.

'Holy Mary, Mother of… a face like that should be on Notre Dame,' said Maguire.

'Tis a look of terror, that's for sure,' said O'Brien. 'Something scared the shite out of him.'

'Would you look at those hands, like feckin' claws, so they are, like he was digging, trying to...'

'Or crawling, maybe,' said O'Brien. 'Crawling, like he was trying to get away.'

Maguire crouched down for a closer look. The deceased was roughly six feet tall, aged about eighty, he guessed, maybe more. The hair, short and grey, was flecked with mud and the eyes, wide open, were a piercing shade of blue. The look of sheer, unadulterated fear, etched deep into the old man's wrinkled, ashen face, gave him the creeps. Apart from the soil which covered his bony hands, there was no sign of a struggle, no torn clothing and no marks or bruises, even his dog collar was intact. He pulled a pair of latex gloves from his jacket, slipped them on and made a cursory search of the deceased's pockets.

'Anything?' asked O'Brien.

'Feck all. Not even a bunch of keys. Wait, here, piece of paper. Bag it, might mean something.'

O'Brien unfolded it.

'Cabrera,' he said. 'Sounds like one of those fancy cars. What do you think it means?'

'You're a feckin' detective, Sergeant, Google it. Find out.'

Maguire stood and slowly surveyed the ground around the corpse.

'See these?' he asked O'Brien. 'They don't belong to this fella.'

O'Brien bent forward to look at the footprints.

'They're in the wrong place and they're flat. Look at the boots on our friend here, commando sole. Make sure forensics have got these covered, photos and a cast if they can.'

'Sir!'

'I want a cause of death as soon as possible and look for anything that shouldn't be there, the usual: hair, bloods, you know the score.'

He peeled off his gloves and sighed.

'Well, that's one less for us to worry about in this Godforsaken bogland,' he muttered.

Shielding his eyes from the low, morning sun, Maguire scanned the horizon for anything incongruous. Anything at all. He nudged O'Brien with his elbow.

'Who's that? That fella there, in the feckin' hedge, thinks he's invisible.'

'Oh him, no idea. Been there all morning, so he has.'

'All morning? And you haven't thought to…?'

Maguire was distracted by a tall figure in a black cassock marching hastily towards them, fists clenched, his gait restricted by the flowing robe. Breathless, he proffered an icy hand.

'I came as soon as I could,' he panted, 'Paddy Brennan, Headmaster. They say you've found a...'

'Yes, we have. D.I. Maguire. This is D.S. O'Brien. Looks like one of yours.'

Maguire stood aside allowing Father Brennan a clear view of the body. Exasperated, he drew a breath and crossed himself.

'Oh, good grief! Why, it's… it's Leo,' he exclaimed, covering his mouth.

'Leo?' asked O'Brien.

'Yes, Father Leo Kavanagh.'

'Well, at least we've an ID,' quipped Maguire. 'Who was he? I mean, in relation to…'

'Headmaster, he was the headmaster here, before me. What happened?'

'Believe it or not,' bemoaned Maguire, 'that's what I've come to find out. Now, tell me, why do you suppose someone would want to kill a priest?'

'Kill? You think he was murdered?' asked Father Brennan.

'Well, unless having a heart attack in a bed of onions at two o'clock in the morning is something he'd planned, I'd say it was a distinct possibility.'

'Murdered?' whispered the headmaster. 'What will the parents say?'

'Is there somewhere we can talk?' asked Maguire. 'Preferably somewhere with four walls and a feckin' roof. Getting a chill, so I am.'

Father Brennan smiled and beckoned him to follow.

'Come so, we'll go to the house, kitchen is toast.'

'Just a minute, Father, that fella there, by the hedge, see, looks like a scarecrow, any ideas?'

The headmaster squinted at the distance.

'Oh, that's Callum,' he said. 'Another one of us, sort of. Brother Callum McGarvey.'

* * *

Maguire sneered at the sheer size of the house. It was more of a mansion, a Victorian pile once home to the landed gentry. Set behind the school, it had, he estimated, at least eight bedrooms, God knows how many bathrooms and, no doubt, a well-stocked wine cellar. The kitchen alone was about the size of the entire ground floor of his two-up, two-down terraced cottage Mrs Maguire referred to as 'quaint'. It was home to Father Brennan, the late Father Kavanagh and a handful of Christian Brothers, all of whom were teachers. As promised, the kitchen was comfortably warm. The housekeeper, Mrs Dooley, abandoned the pots on the range cooker and welcomed them with a pot of tea and a large plate of biscuits.

'Oh, Father, I've just cleaned the floor,' she said, 'will you leave your shoes at the door, there.'

'Sorry, Mrs Dooley, didn't realise it was so muddy out there,' he replied.

'Before we sit down, Father,' said Maguire, 'do you mind if the sergeant here takes a look at Leo's, I mean Father Leo's, room. Just a formality, you understand?'

'Of course not, go right ahead, Mrs Dooley will take you.'

Maguire shed his coat and sat with an exhausted sigh as the headmaster poured each of them a brew.

'This'll perk you up, Inspector,' said Father Brennan.

'That's welcome, so it is. Now, tell me about Father Leo,' he said, 'how's he been, in himself? I mean, did you notice anything odd about him recently, anything at all? A change in his behaviour, perhaps?'

Father Brennan shook his head.

'Can't say I have, we'd see each other every day so if something was up, I'm sure I'd have spotted it.'

'Fair enough, he didn't mention anything to you, didn't…'

'Leo hardly spoke, in fact, he was a man of few words, Inspector, well-liked but he kept himself to himself.'

'What about this Callum fella, then, does he not live here too?'

'Brother Callum left the house many years ago. He's still a Brother, he still has his faith, but he lives alone, over the way there.'

Maguire sipped his tea.

'Why so? Is he not a teacher like the rest of you?'

'He is, or should I say, was, and by all accounts, a very good one at that,' said Father Brennan. 'Let's just say he and Father Leo, God rest his soul, didn't quite see eye to eye.'

'Go on,' said Maguire.

'Well, Inspector, in Father Leo's day this school was, shall we say, a dumping ground for miscreants, misfits and trouble-makers. I believe the phrase they use these days is 'maladjusted'. Leo ruled it with a rod of iron, he thought the only way to educate a boy was to beat it into him. Which he did, frequently.'

'And Callum disapproved?' asked Maguire, helping himself to a biscuit.

'Vehemently. More often than not, he was the one who cleaned up after Leo.'

Maguire sat back and folded his arms.

'And no-one thought to report any of this, this *abuse*, to the authorities?'

The headmaster laughed quietly and smiled.

'Come now, Inspector, I don't have to tell you how Catholic schools were run back in the day. Hear no evil, see no evil. Anyway, Callum advocated a gentler approach, he befriended the boys and nurtured them, even got a couple into university, so he did. He was an innovator, always thinking of new ways to get the lads interested in something. Take the allotment, you know, the vegetable plot, out there in the field, that was originally Callum's idea, to get the lads interested in agriculture.'

'Originally? You mean…'

'Leo refused point blank to let him do it. As far as Callum was concerned, that was the final straw. He tried getting a transfer to another school but there was nothing going, so he quit, packed his bags and left.'

Maguire looked perplexed.

'You're telling me he left because he wasn't allowed to plant a few spuds? I don't get it.'

'The spuds, if you like, were just the icing on the cake. You have to understand, Inspector, the tension between Leo and Callum had grown over many years, it was so deep rooted, it was almost electric. Their situation was, at best, feudal and Callum was nothing but a serf, he had no say in anything. In the end, I think it was sheer frustration that drove him away.'

'Well how come there's a…'

'Vegetable plot now?' said Father Brennan. 'Leo instigated it not long after Callum left, had the boys working like dogs, so he did. They were at it for weeks on end till eventually they grew enough to become self-sufficient. And Callum, poor Callum, he could do nothing but watch. It was like someone had stolen his thunder.'

'And that doesn't strike you as odd, Father?' asked Maguire 'I mean, an ex-teacher, lurking in the hedges, spying...'

'Callum's an old man, Inspector, there's not a bad bone in his body. The only crime he's guilty of is liberating the odd onion now and then. And he's welcome to them.'

'If you don't mind me saying so, Father, you seem to know an awful lot about the history of this school, I mean, the teachers, like.'

The headmaster stretched his arms and grinned boyishly.

'I am proud to say, Inspector, that I was once a pupil here.'

'A pupil? Really? How so?' asked Maguire, surprised, 'I wouldn't have thought this school would've been top of the list for parents back then.'

'I didn't know my parents, I was an orphan.'

'Forgive me for asking but, if you witnessed all that stuff going on, why on earth would you want to come back?'

The headmaster folded his arms and looked skyward.

'Not sure,' he said. 'Fate, I suppose. When the time came to leave I had two choices: go to the labour exchange and forge out a career as a navvy or join the church. It was an easy choice. I went straight to the seminary at St. Vincent's and once I was ordained, well, that was it. I spent a year in the parish then applied for the role as chaplain here. After that, things just happened, before I knew it, I was the Head.'

'With a nice, big house and some pocket money too.'

O'Brien returned clutching a clear, plastic bag containing two large books.

'Father Brennan, would you mind if we borrowed these?' he said, placing them on the table. 'They're Father Leo's diaries, I think they're worth a look.'

The headmaster pushed a cup of tea towards O'Brien.

'Of course, now you best drink that before you go.'

'Thanks. I'll return them as soon we're done,' said O'Brien. 'Say, that's a nasty wee scratch you have on your cheek, there, Father. How'd you get that?'

The headmaster raised his hand and traced it with his middle finger.

'Outside, the brambles I imagine, or one of the rose bushes. Lethal, so they are.'

Maguire stood and pulled on his overcoat.

'Thanks for your time Father, you've been most accommodating, so you have.'

'You're welcome, anytime, Inspector,' said the headmaster.

Maguire grabbed the sergeant by the elbow as they closed the door.

'Shoes,' he whispered, holding a finger to his lips.

'What?'

'Shoes. Bag his shoes, quick.'

'Why?'

Maguire dragged O'Brien away from the door.

'Look at your feckin' shoes, are they muddy?'

'No.'

'Mine?'

'No.'

'Why? Because the ground's feckin' frozen, that's why. So how come he has mud on his? And it's almost dry, so he must've been out here before the frost came down.'

'Right so.'

'Hold on,' said Maguire. 'Two minutes.'

He went back to the kitchen.

'Sorry, Father, nearly forgot, you wouldn't happen to know if Father Leo was planning a trip at all?'

'At his age? I should think not.'

'Not even a wee holiday, Italy maybe?'

'Italy? You mean the Vatican?'

'No, some place called Cabrera.'

O'Brien pulled a bag from his coat pocket and showed the piece of paper to the headmaster.

'Where did you find that?' he asked, hesitantly.

'Not important.'

'Well, it's strange,' said Father Brennan, 'because so far as I know, Cabrera's not a place, Inspector, it's a name.'

'A name? Who's name?' asked Maguire.

'Father Constantine Cabrera. He came here from Spain and taught under Father Leo. Probably the most popular teacher this school's ever seen, but that was years ago, I mean, *years.*'

Maguire frowned and scratched the back of his head.

'Now why,' he began, muttering under his breath, 'why would he be carrying a piece of paper… is he still alive, do you know, this Cabrera fella? Would you have an address for him?'

Father Brennan pursed his lips and raised his eyebrows apologetically.

'He *is* still alive,' he said, 'and *I do* have an address for him, but unfortunately I don't think you'll get much out of him.'

'How so?' asked O'Brien.

'He's in the asylum, at Carlow. Been there, oh, must be forty years now, probably more.'

'Forty years? In the asylum?' asked Maguire 'Why? Is he…?'

'Who knows, Inspector. Some say he had a gift, a second sight, like a visionary. Others say he just went mad.'

11

Chapter 2

Saleres was peaceful. Clinging to the slopes of the Lecrin Valley, halfway between Granada and Salobrena, the tiny village had no shops, no bars and no school, just a church and a dwindling population of devoted farmers. Whitewashed houses, their windows shuttered against the sun, lined the narrow, winding streets. Feral cats, seeking shade from the sweltering heat, lay strewn across the doorways and Father Constantine Cabrera watched from the roof as an old man and his mule patiently climbed the terraces on the opposite side of the vale with steadfast resolve. He scribbled a note for his sermon on Sunday: *'And let us not grow weary of doing good, for in due season we will reap, if we do not give up.'* Galatians 6:9.

* * *

Rest. That was their advice, or rather the Archbishop's. Plenty of rest. He'd concluded that the young Cabrera's docile disposition was not suited to city life and if he remained much longer it would have a detrimental effect on his health. There was too much temptation, too many bars and too many women. It was obviously exhausting him, addling his mind. Concerned for his welfare, they delivered an ultimatum: accept the post in Saleres or seek medical help for his recurring nightmares. Medical help which would entail a lengthy stay in hospital. In reality, they had conspired against him. They considered him a maverick and disliked everything about him, from his rakish appearance to his enviable popularity with the worshippers. That, and the fact that he was incorruptible.

Father Cabrera welcomed his exile. His arrival in the valley raised more than few eyebrows. He was young, tall and good looking, the complete opposite of his predecessor but within days he'd been made as welcome as a prodigal. Life in the valley was simple and rewarding. His official responsibilities included celebrating mass each evening at six o'clock and Sundays at noon, conducting weddings or baptisms should the occasion ever arise and, occasionally, laying someone to rest, usually only after their third heart attack. Apart from that, his time was his own, spent, more often than not, lending his brawn to help with the harvests and teaching the primary school kids in Restábal a couple of afternoons per week.

* * *

Cabrera stuffed his notebook, sketch pad, bible and a poor man's picnic into a knapsack and set off to work on his sermon. Down through the quiet streets, across the Rio Santo and up through the groves, his senses overwhelmed with the scent of oranges and lemons. From the summit he could see everything: his house opposite, Albunuelas to the left, Restábal to right, the river below and a lone eagle gliding on the thermals overhead.

'La vista de Dios,' he sighed. 'La vista de Dios.'

With his sermon more or less complete, he sat back, pulled some manchego from his knapsack, sliced it with a pocket knife and devoured it with a chunk of bread. A hundred feet below, somewhat shaded by the trees, he could just make out an old man harvesting his fruit, methodically placing the oranges, one by one, into the wicker baskets hanging from the mule's back. It was a laborious process, unchanged in centuries, but one that could be hastened with an extra pair of hands. Gingerly, he scrambled down the narrow, overgrown path towards them. He shook his head and sniggered at his own ineptitude, astounded that he could have arrived at the wrong grove from such a short distance. The man and his mule were nowhere to be seen. The land was barren, the trees, dead. He ambled home and prepared for evening mass.

* * *

The ancient and unassuming church of Santiago Apóstol was tucked away in the middle of the village. The doors were seldom locked but each evening at 6 p.m., as the bell chimed solemnly from the tower, the faithful would gather outside the main doors and wait for Father Cabrera to arrive before entering. One by one, he'd shake their hands, enquire about their health, then usher them inside. Apart from Sundays, when the church was full to overflowing, the congregation was rarely large, had an average age of ninety and was almost exclusively female.

That evening the worshippers numbered about a dozen. They sat in private prayer and mumbled their responses in unison, crossing their foreheads at every opportunity. Midway through mass, two latecomers slipped silently into the church. It was La Señora Vega and, he assumed, her son. She was sprightly for a seventy-five-year-old, the eyes and ears of the village, opinionated and brazenly vocal in her beliefs. Cabrera winced. She was the only person in Saleres who had not warmed to the charms of El Padre. With his shoulder length, jet black hair and goatee beard, he had, she often intoned, more in common with 'un gitano' than a man of the cloth. The young Señor Vega, stocky in build with a scar on his left cheek, clutched his cap in both hands and stood behind her. Cabrera caught his eye, smiled politely and bowed his head. He obviously had work to do, by the time the mass was over, he was gone.

The sun was barely over the snow-capped peaks of the Sierra Nevada but already it was hot. By nine o'clock it would be 30°C in the shade. Cabrera, in shirt sleeves and slacks, sat in solitude on the roof and savoured the stillness of the morning. Coffee in hand, he stared contentedly towards Albunuelas, mesmerised by the changing colours of the valley. Somewhere down below, a mule brayed. He leapt to his feet and there he saw them, the old man and his trusty companion, slowly weaving their way up the hillside. Like an excited schoolboy, he dashed from the house, sprinted through the deserted streets, over the Rio Santo and up the path, his feet slipping on the dry, dusty earth. He caught sight of them turning the corner, not fifteen yards ahead. Grinning mischievously, he paused for breath, dusted himself down and went to greet them. His face dropped.

'Soy loco!' he gasped.

The grove was as it was the day before. The ground barren, the trees dead. The old man and his mule were nowhere to be seen. He ran further up the path. Nothing.

He turned and retraced his steps, there was just the one set of footprints. His own. Bewildered, he took a handkerchief from his pocket, wiped his furrowed brow and sat in quiet contemplation. He closed his eyes and listened: the only sound was the distant babble of the Santo as it flowed gently towards Restábal.

* * *

Javier Morales, like Father Cabrera, was a saviour. Without him, half the valley would be as dry as the Santo during a drought and the old men would have nowhere to go to escape their wives and knock back shots of Veterano. 'Bar Morales' was considered by some to be more important than the church. With sweat streaming down his face and his shirt struggling to remain fastened around his ample waist, he clumped down the path, shotgun in one hand, a hessian sack in the other.

'Constantine!' he yelled.

Cabrera looked round and raised a hand in recognition. The sack hit the floor with a thump.

'Been shopping?' he jibed.

Javier smiled as he settled next to Cabrera.

'Rabbit. If you come for lunch, it will be stew; tonight, tapas.'

'And tomorrow?'

'Tomorrow, it will be a distant memory.'

Javier lay back and stared at the cloudless sky.

'Look at that. Beautiful,' he said. 'Every day is beautiful. I don't know what they see in it.'

'Who? What?' asked Cabrera.

'The kids. Granada. Barcelona. As soon they're old enough, they leave.'

'Times are changing, Javier. They don't want to become old farmers, they want to better themselves. Get a good job. Earn good money.'

'Ha! Who needs money. Everything you need is here. I could never leave here. Don't you miss home, Constantine? Where is home?'

Cabrera stared pensively across the valley.

'This is my home now,' he said. 'It used to be Almeria.'

'Almeria? And you don't want to go back?'

'There's nothing for me there, now.'

'Familia?'

'They were killed, in the civil war,' said Cabrera.

'I'm sorry.'

'So am I. I could have saved them.'

'Saved them? What do you mean?' asked Javier.

Cabrera paused before answering.

'The night before they died, I had a dream. I dreamt I saw them in our church, the Iglesia de San Roque, cowering for some reason, between the pews. They were with the priest and two other people I didn't recognise. Then the ceiling fell, huge blocks of stone plummeted to the ground. There was dust and screaming and then I awoke. I said nothing.'

He turned to face Javier.

'The following day, it was a Monday, just after dawn, my parents were on their way to work when a German battleship began bombarding Almeria. They ran to the church, for safety. Two hundred missiles hit Almeria that day. Much of the town, and the church, was destroyed.

'I never knew. Constantine, I'm sorry…'

'Gracias, Javier, but don't be sorry. Everything happens for a reason, you see, if they hadn't died, I wouldn't have found God. If I hadn't found God, I wouldn't have joined the church, and if I hadn't joined the church, I wouldn't be here now, sitting with you.'

Javier laughed.

'And I would be in the kitchen, skinning rabbits instead of sitting on my culo talking to a priest! Tell me, then, what brought you here, to the valley?'

'Not what, Javier, who.'

'I don't understand.'

'Let's just say my superiors in Granada didn't like... they didn't like my beard.'

* * *

Cabrera left Javier with a smirk on his face and headed for Restábal. His was the first lesson of the afternoon at the school on Calle San José where most of the kids from the valley were educated until the age of twelve. He was greeted with the usual cheering and shouting by the enthusiastic niños, eager to hear another of his tales. Unlike the other teachers, he spurned the desk and chose instead to sit, cross-legged, on the floor. The children gathered round him in a semi-circle.

'Sometimes,' he said, 'you have to expect the unexpected. Sometimes, you may have to do things you weren't prepared for, and sometimes, a miracle may happen.'

The kids, enthralled, listened in silence as he told of a wedding at Cana in Galilee and how everyone was having a swinging time until, that is, the wine ran out. The guests were annoyed, there wasn't a bar nearby, like the one in Albunuelas, so Jesus' mother told him to get on the case.

18

"Woman," he said, "why do you involve me? My hour has not yet come." Seeing the look of disappointment on all the guests' faces, he reluctantly told the servants to fill all the stone jars with water and take them to master of the banquet. This they did and when the master tasted it, he said "This wine is superb! Why did you save the best till last?" The kids cheered with delight.

'Now,' said Cabrera, 'something else unexpected, let's have some fun.'

He handed every child a sheet of plain, white paper.

'Who can tell me what real wine is made from?' he asked.

Twenty hands shot in the air, 'La uva!' they cried in unison.

'La uva!' said Cabrera 'Grapes! Correct! Now, I want you all to draw a picture of something else that grows in the valley, anything at all.'

Fifteen minutes later the children downed pencils and jostled for the chance to be the first to show their masterpieces to the rest of the class. One by one, they stood.

'Naranja. Very good,' said Cabrera. 'And next, El pero. Well, yes, I suppose we do have dogs growing in the valley, just like the rest of us. What else? Limon, Aceituna…' Last to show was a small boy at the back of the class. He looked tired and drawn.

'Don't be shy!' said Cabrera 'I'm sure it's very good, whatever it is, let's see!'

The boy stood and held aloft a magnificent rendering of two fruit on a stalk.

'La cereza,' he whispered.

'Cherries!' said Cabrera, 'and what amazing cherries they are, well done!'

* * *

The following morning, Cabrera packed his knapsack and made his way to the summit on the opposite side of the valley. For three hours, he sat in quiet solitude and sketched the Sierras to the east and the village of Restábal lying dormant in their shadow. Once embellished with inks and water colours, he would take them to the market in Lanjaron to sell. It was an easy way to supplement his income and the money raised would be enough to buy more paper and pencils for the kids at the school. A car horn sounded as he closed his pad. He could just make out the small, white van winding its way through the streets of Saleres. 'Fish,' he told himself, fresh from the harbour at Motril. As he packed his bag he caught a fleeting glimpse of a mule, tail swishing, in the campo below. He considered following when a voice disturbed him. A low, gruff voice so close it caused him to jump.

'Toma,' it said.

Cabrera, shocked by his sudden appearance, turned to face a burly, young man who stood, smiling, with a glint in his eye. He recognised him instantly, it was the young man from the church, the son of La Señora Vega. He held, in his hand, a palmful of cherries.

'*¡Toma!*'

Warily, Cabrera took one and savoured it. It was the ripest, sweetest cherry he had ever tasted.

'Muchas gracias,' he enthused, hesitating before taking another. 'Tell me, the old man and his mule,' he said, pointing down the valley. '*¿Has visto el hombre con el mulo?*'

20

The young man shook his head and laughed quietly.

'No hay hombre con la mulo,' he whispered.

Cabrera smiled and shook his head.

'Yes there is, I saw them. You must have seen them too,' he said.

Señor Vega looked him in the eye.

'Es el espiritu del valle,' he said as he left. '*El espiritu.*'

Cabrera dropped his bag and lit a cigarette. Drawing heavily, he pondered the young man's word. It unnerved him.

* * *

The bell fell silent and the crowd grew restless. It was not like El Padre to be late. The swifts and the swallows swooped overhead as he ran into the square, smiling apologetically.

'Lo siento,' he said as he herded them inside. 'Lo siento.'

On the bench, by the shade of the trees, sat an elderly man. Despite the weather, he wore, as did most octogenarians, a thick, tweed jacket over a shirt and jumper and a flat, woollen cap. He tapped his cane on the ground.

'Señor Barbo!' exclaimed Cabrera. 'Didn't see you hiding there! To what do I owe this pleasure?'

'Pleasure?' he scowled. 'What pleasure do you get from seeing an old man who can hardly walk?'

'I get pleasure from seeing an old man who likes to talk,' said Cabrera.

El Barbo regarded him closely.

'You have bags under your eyes. Something troubles you?' he asked.

Cabrera hesitated and sat beside him.

21

'This afternoon,' he said quietly, 'I saw, I thought I saw...' he paused and tapped El Barbo on the knee. 'It's alright, doesn't matter. I'm just a little tired, I think. Are you coming in?'

'I'm resting, Padre. I get enough sermons at home. See you on Sunday.'

Cabrera returned to his congregation and rattled off the mass in Latin. It was something the ladies enjoyed, somehow it made the whole experience even more religious. Thirty minutes later they filed, one by one, from the church. Last to leave was the diminutive La Señora Vega. Father Cabrera took a deep breath and approached her warily.

'Señora Vega, ¿como estas?' he enquired with a tilt of the head.

'Soy bien, Padre, soy bien,' she replied, sternly.

'I was hoping to catch you, I wanted to thank your son for the cherries.'

'My son?' she asked, taken aback.

'Si, this afternoon, en el arboleda, we met and he gave me some cherries. Truly, the best...'

'And you are sure it was my son?' she huffed.

'Of course, I'm positive.'

La Señora Vega beat her chest with a clenched fist, opened her purse and thrust a small, black and white photo under his nose.

'Is this the man you saw?' she scowled, now agitated.

'Yes, your son, look, the scar on his cheek, the hair parted on the...'

The old lady snatched the photo from his hands and returned it to her purse.

'Padre Cabrera,' she growled, her mood erupting, 'this is not funny. My son died twenty-seven years ago! 27 years! If you want to see his tomb, he lies in the cemetery at Albunuelas. Go see for yourself!'

Cabrera, stunned into silence, watched dumbfounded as she stormed up the street.

'*Died?*' he mumbled under his breath, '*but the cherries, I ate...*'

He clasped his hands beneath his chin, closed his eyes and whispered a prayer.

* * *

The walk to Albunuelas, uphill but pleasant enough in the warm evening air, took little more than half an hour. He paused anxiously outside the cemetery and continued on his way. Javier, perched precariously atop an empty keg, was pruning the vine above the entrance to the bar.

'Hola!' said Cabrera as he breezed by. Javier jumped down and followed him inside.

'Hola, Constantine! You're too late, the rabbit is just a delicious memory!'

'I'm not hungry, Javier.'

'Are you sure? I can get you some jamon, if you like.'

'No. Gracias.'

'¿Cerveza?' he asked.

'Si, grande, y cigarrillos.'

Javier slid an ice-cold glass of Alhambra across the bar and slammed down a pack of Ducados. Cabrera drank half the glass without pausing and lit a cigarette.

'Something on your mind, Padre?' asked Javier. 'You seem jumpy.'

Cabrera drew hard on his cigarette and blew the smoke towards the ceiling. He regarded Javier with a look of consternation.

'La Señora Vega, how many children did she have?' he asked.

'One. A son.'

'You're sure? Not two; brothers, perhaps?'

'No,' said Javier. 'Definitely one.'

'Any other family? Nephews? Cousins?'

'How many times? No! She is all alone, why, what's bothering you?'

Cabrera knocked back the beer and nodded as he pushed the glass towards Javier.

'I saw him. This afternoon, after you left. I saw her son, up in the groves.'

'Impossible, Constantine, simply impossible!' said Javier, passing him another beer. 'He died years ago, thirty years ago, maybe more. Very sad, so young, not even married. They say he had a weak heart.'

Cabrera lit another cigarette.

'¡No entiendo!' he mumbled.

'Perhaps it was someone else, you're just mistaken.'

'Perhaps you're right, Javier,' said Cabrera, downing his beer. 'Perhaps you're right. Hasta luego.'

* * *

It must have been someone else, it was the only rational explanation, someone who looked remarkably like the young Señor Vega, someone who came from Restábal, perhaps, or Melegis, but still, it made no sense and did nothing to relieve his anxiety. It was four o'clock in the morning, Cabrera became increasingly distressed as he tried to rationalise the encounter with the young Señor

Vega and the way he dismissed the sighting of the old man and his mule. Agitated, he left the house, hurried through the darkness, over the river and up the valley to the summit. There he lay, surrounded by the sound of chirping crickets, till the sun climbed over the mountains. He hadn't slept, nor had he washed or shaved. His shirt, damp with dew, clung to his back. He sat up, peeled an orange and waited. By the time they'd arrived, he'd almost exhausted the pack of Ducados and consumed a week's worth of vitamin C. The mule, stock still, stood quietly as the old man filled the baskets atop its back with the fragrant, ripe fruit. Two hours later, task completed, they began their descent. Cabrera, wary of spooking his quarry, followed discreetly. He watched as the farmer tethered his mule to the bridge across the Santo and patted it lovingly on the head. Cabrera smiled.

'¡Por fin!' he said as he dipped his head and lit a final cigarette.

His delight turned to despair.

'¿Dónde está el hombre?' he yelled, running towards the bridge. '¿Dónde está el hombre con el mulo?'

El Molinero, disturbed by the shouting, ran from the mill to find Cabrera spinning on his heels, arms flailing.

'¿Qué pasa? Padre, *¿qué pasa?*' he asked.

Cabrera held his head in his hands, his face tortured with distress.

'Where are they?' he pleaded 'You saw them, you must have seen them, they were right here, the old man and his mule, he tied it to the bridge!'

The miller walked towards him, laughing.

'Padre, there must be at least a dozen mules in Saleres, which one in particular are you looking for!'

Cabrera, despondent, collapsed on the bench.

'I have seen no-one, Padre,' said the miller, placing an arm on his shoulder, 'not a soul, and I have been here all morning.'

'But I followed them, I followed them down from the grove, he stopped right there and…'

'Wait here, one moment.'

The miller returned with a cup of water.

'Here, drink this. Hoy es muy caliente, I think the sun has got to you.'

'It's not the sun! I saw them! They were right here!'

The miller smiled reassuringly.

'Of course they were, Padre. I believe you. Tell me, what did they look like?' he asked.

Cabrera lolled back his head and closed his eyes.

'The mule was, *beautiful*,' he said. 'White, white with a tan blaze, here, down his nose, and the man, *gentle*. He looked so, *so contented*, so, *at peace*. He wore a hat, a straw hat, he was shorter than me, about five six, and around his neck…'

'Around his neck, he wore a red bandana,' said the miller.

Cabrera sat up with a jolt.

'Yes!' he exclaimed 'How did you know? You did see them!'

The miller looked to the ground and rubbed the back of his neck. He spoke in barely more than a whisper.

'The man you describe, Padre,' he said, 'is Señor Garcia Del Soto.'

Cabrera leapt to his feet and laughed aloud.

'Garcia Del Soto! I knew it! I knew I wasn't seeing things!' he said, clapping his hands 'So tell me, this Garcia Del Soto, where does he live?'

El Molinero looked skyward and hesitated before answering.

'Con los estrellas,' he said forlornly.

Cabrera dropped his arms and walked slowly towards the miller.

'What?' he said 'I don't understand, what do you mean, *with the stars?*'

'Ven conmigo.'

The miller led Cabrera across the bridge and pointed to a small, stone plaque by the bank. It read: '*En memoria de Garcia Del Soto*'.

'There was a storm,' he said, 'twelve years ago, a mighty storm. The Santo burst its banks, every bridge from here to Melegis was wiped out. He drowned, right here, trying to get home. His mule perished with him.'

Cabrera sank to his knees and crossed himself.

'Santa Madre,' he whispered. 'Help me.'

* * *

Fearful he was losing his mind, Cabrera slid slowly into depression. A week went by, then two. It was long enough for the villagers to start talking, or more precisely, the women. 'El Padre does not sleep' they said, 'El Padre has lost weight.' 'El Padre is ill.' His goatee had transformed into a full grown beard, his unruly hair became a mass of tangled of knots and his cassock bore evidence of the previous day's meal. Even celebrating mass became an effort. Unable to concentrate, it evolved into nothing more than half an hour of incoherent rambling, peppered with the occasional smile, given as some kind of reassurance that all was well. The only person to delight in his unstable condition was La Señora Vega.

'What do you expect from un gitano?' she hissed.

Though his state of mind was faltering, the support from the village did not. The ladies would pass him on the street, say nothing, but pat him reassuringly on the arm. Each morning he would leave the house to find a pan on the doorstep containing a fresh tortilla. When he returned there'd be a large pot of 'patatas a lo pobre', or 'olla podrida' waiting for him. '*Perhaps this is the spirit of the valley,*' he thought.

* * *

Señor Barbo was sitting outside the church. His wrinkled face creased with a smile as the dishevelled Cabrera joined him. They sat together and enjoyed a cigarette. Señor Barbo, hands resting on his cane, gaze fixed dead ahead, spoke quietly.

'La Señora Vega is travelling to Granada next week,' he said.

'A holiday?' asked Cabrera.

'No. She is visiting an acquaintance. A man.'

'A man? At her age?' quipped Cabrera.

El Barbo smiled.

'He works at the Cathedral de Santa Maria.'

'What does he do?'

Señor Barbo paused deliberately.

'The same as you.'

Cabrera said nothing as the old man heaved himself from the bench.

'Life is good here, Padre,' he said. 'Better than a hospital.'

There were two orange trees, one for the old man and one for the mule. Around them, twelve lemon trees, one for each of the years since his untimely demise. The grove that had once belonged to Garcia Del Soto was breathing again. It had taken Cabrera two whole weeks to clear it and prepare the soil, and another to plant the poles. The afternoon sun bore down on his back as he gathered up the last of the dead wood. Finally, head bowed, he said a silent prayer and blessed the ground. His ears pricked at the sound of bottles clinking somewhere along the path. Javier appeared and held aloft a small crate of beer.

'I think you've earned one of these,' he said. 'Maybe two!'

They sat together and admired the grove.

'Garcia would've liked this,' said Javier. 'You must be proud.'

'I am proud only of God,' said Cabrera. 'He gave me the ability to do this.'

'Self-deprecating too!'

Javier swigged his beer and leaned back on his elbows.

'You're looking well, Constantine. That big beard didn't suit you! Are you feeling better now?' he asked.

'Gracias, yes, much better,' said Cabrera with an appreciative smile.

'No more, *visitors with cherries?* Old men harvesting their…'

Cabrera laughed and shook his head.

'No, no more visitors,' he said.

* * *

It was late. The smell of smoke filled the air as Cabrera, weary from toiling in the campo, snuffed out the candles. The door creaked opened behind him. He turned to face an elderly man silhouetted in the moonlight.

'Señor Barbo,' he said quietly, with a smile.

'Is it too late, Padre?'

'It's never too late, Señor, come,' said Cabrera, beckoning him with a wave of the arm.

The old man shuffled towards him and perched on the end of a pew.

'I hear you have planted Del Soto's grove,' he said.

Cabrera nodded.

'Oranges and lemons,' he said. 'Lest we should forget.'

'He will not forget. He thanks you.'

'I'm sure he does,' said Cabrera, 'but tell me, why so late, Señor? Can I help you with something?'

'Will you hear my confession, Padre?' asked Señor Barbo.

'Of course.'Cabrera left the old man to recite his penance in peace. Outside, he sat beneath a crescent moon, lit a cigarette and waited. An elderly lady hurried into the square, a look of angst on her face.

'Señora Barbo!' he exclaimed, rising to greet her. 'Don't look so worried, he's here, inside!'

'What are you talking about, Padre? Who is inside?'

'Your husband, of course.'

La Señora Barbo scowled at the priest.

'Have you lost your mind? He's at home, he's been in bed all day! You must come at once, Padre, he hasn't long, come now!'

Cabrera threw down his cigarette and dashed inside the church. It was empty. His head twitched and a cold sweat trickled down the back of his neck. He locked arms with the old lady and escorted her, as fast as possible, back to the house. They climbed the stairs to the bedroom on the first floor and, cautiously, he eased back the door. There, lying on his back with a look of serene contentment on his face, was Señor Barbo. There was a dull thud as Cabrera's knees hit the stone floor. Through gritted teeth, he rapidly recited a prayer for the repose of the old man's soul, blessed him and left.

It was five o'clock in the evening. Cabrera's hands shook as he sipped a glass of Tempranillo. He hadn't slept and he hadn't eaten. The door remained locked. Fearful of who, or what he might see, he chose to remain indoors. Nervously, he checked his watch. In less than an hour, he had to celebrate mass. He paced the room, anxious at the thought of going out, when there came a knock at the door. He froze, confused, unsure of what to do. They knocked again. He ran his fingers through his hair, took a deep breath and yanked open the door. La Señora Barbo stood before him, hands clasped beneath her breast. She looked deep into his sallow eyes and smiled.

'Señora,' said Cabrera, his mouth twitching towards a smile. 'How nice to see you. How are you…?'

She regarded him reassuringly.

'Esto es para ti,' she said, holding out her hand. Wrapped around her fingers was a small medallion hanging on a chain. 'He wanted you to have it. He said you'd know what to do.'

Cabrera laid the trinket in the palm of his hand.

'What do you mean?' he whispered.

'I have no idea, Padre. The old fool always talked in riddles. All I know is, it belonged to his great grandfather. He was from Irlanda.'

'Irlanda? No, I cannot take this, Señora, really, you must…'

'I won't hear of it,' she said, closing his hand around the medal, 'take it.'

Cabrera skipped the pleasantries and hurried past the congregation which had gathered outside the church. Their welcoming smiles, fearing he'd relapsed, dropped at the sight of his pained expression, the stubble on his chin and the yellow tinge in his eyes. Stupefied by his agitated state, their mood soon became sombre and funereal. Breathless, he mumbled his way through the service without looking up and, forsaking the idle banter which usually followed, hastened from the church and left them gossiping in his wake.

* * *

It was peaceful in the grove. Bathed in the soft evening sunshine, he wandered slowly, from tree to tree, touching each one with his fingertips. He paused at the orange blossom. As he brushed it, a single, white petal fluttered to the ground and settled on a hoof print. Cabrera smiled broadly.

'Hola, Garcia,' he whispered.

He reached into his pocket and pulled out the medallion. The tarnished gold glistened in the sun. It was small, just a half an inch across. On one side was a worn engraving of a man's profile, on the other, he could just make out the words: 'Saint Jerome Emiliani. Patron Saint of Abandoned Children'.

The following evening an anxious crowd gathered outside the door to his house. It was eight o'clock, Cabrera had not been seen all day and, to cap it all, he'd missed mass. Rumours of his demise were rife. La Señora Vega smiled smugly while the other women snuffled, inconsolably, into their handkerchiefs.

Chapter 3

Maguire was flummoxed. A body with a knife in the back was easy. A Jesuit with dirt beneath his nails and a face like a gargoyle was a different kettle of fish altogether. He patted his burgeoning belly as it growled uncontrollably.

'What kept you? I'm feckin' starving,' he said as O'Brien burst through the door.

'Sorry, sir, had something to do.'

'Did you bring my sandwich?' asked Maguire.

'Aye, here you go, two toasted bacon, white bread, brown sauce. Nice and healthy.'

'You've a cheek. Eat any more of that feckin' bird seed and you'll grow a beak, so you will. What kept you?'

'Had to get a card for Gráinne, it's her birthday tomorrow,' said O'Brien.

Maguire raised his eyes to the heavens and shook his head.

'No doubt you've something sickeningly sentimental planned for her.'

O'Brien smiled as he shovelled a mouthful of cous-cous into his gob.

'Maybe. You telling me you never treat your wife?'

Maguire choked on his sandwich.

'Treat her well enough, so I do. She's well looked after, is Mrs Maguire, no doubt about that,' he said. 'Last year I booked three weeks in the Isle of Skye.'

'I don't recall you going to the Isle of Skye.'

'I didn't. She did. Feckin' bliss, so it was. Pass my tea. Now, have you found anything on this McGarvey fella?'

'Nothing,' said O'Brien, 'he's clean as a whistle.'

'I still think there's something creepy about him, we'll have a chat, so we will. What about Father Leo?' asked Maguire. 'I couldn't find anything about this so-called abuse, you know, the beatings and the like. I'm beginning to wonder if it's true.'

'I'm with you there. If everything I've read about Kavanagh is to be believed, he'll be canonised before the week is out. Born in Wicklow, only child of Eileen Brennan and Colm Kavanagh. His father was a lay preacher. Parents both died before his sixteenth birthday.'

'Did you check his medical records?'

'I did that.'

'And there was nothing about mental illness?'

'No,' said O'Brien with a smirk. 'Why do you think he has a history of mental illness?'

'Because, I can think of no other reason to be digging in a feckin' vegetable plot at two in the morning with an arctic breeze blowing up your cassock. You'd have to be loopy.'

O'Brien laughed.

'I still say he was trying to get away, escape. I reckon someone had him by the ankles and he was clawing at the ground to break free.'

Maguire slurped his tea and shook his head disparagingly.

'You youngsters,' he said, 'use a bit of common sense. If that was so, all he had to do was grab an onion and whop the fella on the head with it. No, he wasn't trying to get away, of that I'm sure.'

'Well,' said O'Brien, 'from where I'm sitting, we only have two credible lines of inquiry.'

'This'll be good,' said Maguire, sitting back with a sardonic smile.

'We're either looking for someone with a grudge against Father Leo.'

'Genius. Or?'

'Or someone with a priest fixation. Someone who has nothing to do with the school or the Jesuits or any of it. An outsider,' said O'Brien.

'An outsider,' said Maguire. 'An outsider who just happens to be in a deserted field in the middle of the night and decides he'll top a priest?'

'He may have been stalking him, and anyways, who says he's the first? We may well be looking for a serial killer.'

Maguire rolled his eyes.

'Have you been sniffing Tippex again? A serial killer? The only serial killer you'll find around here is someone who's killed a packet of corn flakes. Come so, finish your Trill, let's go to Carlow, have a chat with this Cabrera fella.'

There was a knock at the door, a sharp, double rap. A Garda breezed in and handed O'Brien a sealed, plastic envelope.

'Just came, sir, by courier,' he said, 'from pathology.'

Maguire waited as O'Brien opened the envelope and flicked through the report on Kavanagh, scanning each page for the salient points.

'Well?' asked Maguire, tapping his fingers.

O'Brien held his hand aloft.

'Hold on, okay, blah, blah, blah, oh, here we go. Acute myocardial infarction and multiple organ failure.'

'Meaning?'

'Meaning something scared the shite out of him. He died of shock, a massive shock. He literally got the fright of his life.'

'That's a great help,' said Maguire. 'I could've told you that when we found him. Come on, Carlow awaits. Have you ever to been to a looney bin before?'

'No, sir, can't say I have.'

'Well, don't wander off, you might not get out.'

* * *

'Holy Mother of God!' said Maguire as they turned off the street. 'How many mad people are there in Ireland? It's feckin' huge.'

The Carlow Asylum was an imposing granite and limestone building set in acres of landscaped grounds. They drove past the manicured lawns, parked the car and wandered up the drive towards the main entrance. O'Brien sneezed as they walked in, the reception stank of disinfectant. Maguire approached the desk with a smile.

'One single and one double, please,' he said. 'And what time do you serve breakfast?'

The receptionist, stony-faced, was unimpressed. Maguire sighed and produced his warrant card.

'D.I. Maguire,' he said. 'This is D.S. O'Brien. We'd like to see Father Constantine Cabrera, please.'

37

'Do you have an appointment?' she asked sternly.

'No, I tried calling him direct but he didn't answer.'

The young lady allowed herself a smirk.

'Take a seat,' she said as she picked up the phone.

Twenty minutes later a bespectacled gent casually dressed in an open-necked shirt and sports jacket approached Maguire and proffered his hand.

'Tom Delaney,' he said. 'Clinical Psychologist, how can I help?'

'D.I. Maguire, we'd like to have a word with Father Cabrera, if that's possible.'

Delaney shook his head.

'Afraid not. Father Cabrera does not have visitors,' he said.

'And why would that be?' asked Maguire, refusing to budge.

'Because, Inspector Maguire... actually, I don't know why. Apart from the fact he's never had any.'

'Never? No-one from the church? Not even a letter?'

Delaney shook his head.

'No. Nothing. Tell you what, I'll take you to him but he'll not speak, mind, he hasn't spoken for twenty years, and that's as long as I've been here. Follow me.'

* * *

Cabrera's cell, or room as it was now called, was in the old wing which, save for new lights and a coat of paint, had remained largely unchanged. They walked the corridor in silence, the only sound, the clacking of their heels on the tiled floor.

'It looks grim, but really, it's not that bad,' said Delaney.

They stopped by a metal door with a window no more than a foot square. Maguire peered inside the cell and drew a breath. The room was small with a concrete floor and a single window set high towards the ceiling. Pushed against one wall was a single bed, opposite, a wash-stand and toilet. Cabrera, wearing just a vest and Y-fronts, sat hunched on a wooden chair. His hair, bound in a pony tail, was halfway down his back. A cigarette clung to his lower lip as he rocked, gently, back and forth. Maguire turned to the doctor.

'I never realised,' he said. 'Is he that bad?'

Delaney smiled apologetically.

'There's nothing we can do for him except keep him happy, if there is such a thing.'

He glanced back. Cabrera spat the cigarette from his lips, extinguished it with his bare foot and lit another.

'Is he violent?' asked Maguire.

'Quite the opposite. He's the epitome of meek, shy even, won't even look at the nurses.'

'What does he do all day?'

'Not much. He gets a bath. Eats his meals, walks about a bit and when the sun goes down, he goes to bed. Come the morning, he returns to the chair.'

'And that's it?' said Maguire. 'That's the sum total of his existence?'

'Pretty much,' said Delaney. 'He used to draw pictures. Not many, I think we have about a dozen on file, but he stopped when we took his pencil away.'

'Why did you do that?'

'Self-harming. He took to stabbing his leg every time he finished a picture.'

'And he never speaks?'

'Never. If you get close enough, you may hear him recite the rosary,' said Delaney, 'but that's it. Just the prayers, over and over and over.'

Maguire rubbed his chin and sighed.

'Tell me, Doctor Delaney, have you any idea why he was sectioned? I mean, someone must've brought him in, is there any...'

'According to the records he experienced some kind of breakdown, that's all we know. Details are a bit thin on the ground I'm afraid, Inspector, it was a long time ago. Look, I don't know if it makes things any easier, but back then people were brought here and locked up for the most ridiculous of reasons.'

'How so?' asked Maguire.

Delaney took a deep breath.

'Well,' he said, 'for example, some folk were locked up for being drunk and disorderly, others for having epilepsy, some because they had a tic, or Tourette's, and quite a few of the women, simply for having a baby outside of marriage.'

'You are feckin' joking me, right?' said Maguire.

'I wish I was,' said Delaney. 'I wish I was.'

O'Brien was staring through the window, transfixed as Cabrera stared back, his penetrating eyes locked on the sergeant's gaze. Maguire nudged him with his elbow.

'You've been quiet so, nothing to add?' he said.

'Can he hear us?' whispered O'Brien.

'Not a word,' said Delaney.

'Why is he staring at me?'

'Because you're telepathetic,' said Maguire.

'Do you think,' asked O'Brien without averting his gaze, 'do you think it's possible this place made him mad?

I mean, that he was kind of, alright, when he came in, but then…'

'It's possible, Sergeant,' said Delaney, 'maybe even likely. They could have given him shock therapy or they could have drugged him up to the eyeballs, either of those could have sent him doolally. Then again, they could've just locked the door and left him to fester. Sadly, we will never know.'

* * *

O'Brien buckled his seatbelt and sighed.

'There but for the grace of God,' he said.

Maguire grinned.

'If I'd known about this place,' he said, 'I wouldn't have bothered with the Isle of Skye.'

Chapter 4

The smell was enough to make him heave, almost. O'Brien held a handkerchief to his nose as he looked around the kitchen. An indeterminable substance only forensics would be able to identify covered the top of the stove. A bottle of something that used to be milk stood on the draining board and, next to it, a half empty tin of baked beans was laid siege by an army of marauding ants. He grimaced at the thought of touching anything for fear of contracting a contagious disease. A pair of well-worn gardening gloves lay discarded on the mat by the back door. He carefully bagged them, shoved them into his pocket and joined Maguire in the living room. Callum, reclining in a winged armchair, was gaunt and frail. A pair of round, wired spectacles were hooked behind his abnormally large ears and the top of his head, hairless and shiny, was spotted with freckles.

'I've not renounced my faith, Inspector, I'm still a Jesuit, I'm still Brother Callum,' he said.

'Well, I'm not here to question your faith, Brother, it's just a few friendly questions, that's all. It's not an interrogation,' said Maguire.

'Right so, how can I help?'

'No doubt you've noticed a little activity going on, in the field, there.'

'I have,' said McGarvey.

'You don't seem surprised. Not even curious?' asked Maguire.

'I'm not one to pry, Inspector. Enlighten me, what did you find?'

'A body.'

'A body? And I thought it was only vegetables they planted.'

'It was Leo Kavanagh.'

Callum sighed.

'Is that so? Well, can't say I'll miss him, but may he rest in peace all the same.'

Maguire shuffled uneasily in his seat, perturbed by McGarvey's lack of interest.

'I understand you two weren't, shall we say, the best of friends,' he said.

'That's an understatement. I hated him. No, that's not true, there was no malice, he was actually quite an affable fella, when he wanted to be. It was his methods I hated.'

'His methods?'

'Kavanagh believed there was only one way to educate a child and that was to beat it into him. He'd have been more suited to running a boxing school,' said McGarvey.

'So he was fond of his fists?'

'Not averse to using the strap too. And the cane, and anything else he could lay his hands on,' said Callum.

43

'Have you any idea why? I mean, why he was so violent?'

'He wasn't violent by nature, Mr Maguire, just towards the children.'

'Right, so, and you thought that was wrong?'

'Wouldn't you?' said McGarvey. 'Anyway, what I thought didn't matter. Leo regarded the kids as an inconvenience, a waste of space, accidents that should never have happened. No-one believed you could find the good in a child by being nice to them.'

'But you did.'

'I did that,' said McGarvey.

'Then why did you leave?' asked Maguire.

'Because, even with the love of God, there's only so much a man can take. Seeing those kids take a beating, day in, day out, and not being able to do a thing about it except clean them up, near enough drove me to depression. I had to leave. For my own sake.'

'You didn't try talking to Leo about it? asked O'Brien. 'See if there was a way you two could...'

'I did once, and got punched for my troubles. Leo Kavanagh would listen to no-one, Sergeant. He was a law unto himself. Will you take some tea? I've a pint of milk left somewhere, I'm sure.'

O'Brien hastily declined.

'What about Father Cabrera?' asked Maguire.

McGarvey's face lit up.

'Ah! Now there's a fella for you!' he said, gleaming enthusiastically. 'Old Constantine, a kinder man, you'd never meet. When he came knocking on our door he could hardly speak a word of English, within a month he was as good as fluent. Remarkable man.'

'You weren't jealous?' asked O'Brien.

'And why would that be?'

'Human nature, I suppose. New fella arrives, breath of fresh air, popular, with the kids, like.'

'Teaching isn't a popularity contest, Inspector, it's like the church, it's a vocation and teaching kids, that was all I ever wanted to do,' said McGarvey.

'And Cabrera? Was he an advocate of Father Leo's methods?' asked Maguire.

'Christ, no. Certainly not. There was something about him, old Constantine. You know, he never raised his hands, nor his voice, not once. He had a way with the kids, it's like they were drawn to him, like a magnet. He was gifted, that's for sure. He could have gone on to greater things.'

'But he,' said Maguire, 'he had, some kind of breakdown, is that right?'

'Who knows. It was Leo who sent him packing, he was convinced he'd gone mad.'

'Father Leo?' asked O'Brien.

'To be sure, packed him off to Carlow. I think he's still there.'

'And no-one went to see him? No-one tried to get him out?'

'With Leo around, no-one would dare,' said McGarvey, 'besides, things were different then, Inspector, if they put you in the asylum, they threw away the keys.'

Chapter 5

Cabrera was exhausted. He travelled light, carrying a grip packed with just a change of clothes, his bible and a razor. The journey had taken four days. Overland by train to Bilbao, twenty-four hours on the ferry to Portsmouth, then across to Pembroke and the ferry to Rosslare. When he arrived in Dublin, he sought help from the clergy at Christ Church Cathedral and together, they spent hours trawling through several directories listing every religious establishment in the country. There was not a single church, nor orphanage, nor hospital in the whole of Ireland that went by the name of Saint Jerome. Just a school. One school. Saint Jerome's School for Boys on the outskirts of Innishannon.

Raindrops clung to the brim of his galero as the storm clouds thickened overhead. Father Cabrera pulled the medallion from around his neck and pressed it gently to his lips. A stone wall, eight feet high, surrounded the sprawling building, rendering it invisible to the outside world. A single, wooden gate marked the entrance from the street. He rang the bell and waited. He rang again.

From beyond the gate came the sound of footsteps storming down a gravel path. A voice boomed as the gate swung open.

'Do you know what feckin' time it is?'

Father Leo Kavanagh stood shivering under an umbrella. His scowl melted at the sight of the dog collar.

'Father?' he said, puzzled by the sudden appearance of a priest on his doorstep.

Cabrera doffed his hat.

'Buenas noches, Señor. Me llamo Cabrera. Padre Cabrera. He venido de Andalucia.'

'What?' exclaimed Leo, even more perplexed. 'Oh look, not here, you'd better come in, follow me.'

* * *

'He's foreign,' said Leo, xenophobically, as he entered the lounge. Brother Callum McGarvey smiled warmly and rose to greet their guest.

'Italiano?' he asked, noting his olive complexion.

Cabrera smiled.

'Español,' he replied.

'Hablo poco español!' beamed Callum. 'Muy poco. Siéntese, por favor.'

Cabrera nodded politely and took a seat.

'You must be hungry, I'll get the housekeeper to make you a sandwich, and some tea. No, coffee, you'll prefer coffee, I'm sure.'

'Si, con leche, gracias,' said Cabrera.

'So tell me, why are you here? Who sent you?' asked Callum.

'Santo Jerome sent me,' said Cabrera. 'I am here to teach for Santo Jerome.'

* * *

Kavanagh sneered at the suggestion.

'Well, we do have a spare room,' said McGarvey. 'And he doesn't want paying. And we could use the help.'

'This is not a hostel, Brother Callum! This is a school, not a halfway house for every Tom, Dick and Spik that decides to drop by unannounced.'

'That's not very Christian of you, Leo. Besides, he's here now, give him a go. If he's useless, I'll tell him to leave.'

'Do you not think it just a little bit suspicious that he wants to teach here? Why, of all the schools in Ireland, did he come to this one?' said Kavanagh.

'He told you,' said Callum. 'Saint Jerome.'

'Saint Jerome my arse. Alright, one month, and if he's shite, he goes.'

* * *

The school was crammed with wayward boys between the ages of five and fifteen, boys who were deemed unteachable or backward and who were, more often than not, illegitimate. Each day began with mass in the school's chapel where Father Leo would deliver sermons laced with fire and brimstone and the threat of eternal damnation should any pupil dare to disobey his commands. Latin, Algebra and Religious Education topped the curriculum with most other subjects deemed surplus to requirements. The consequences for arriving late for lessons, or failing to attend at all, were not worth contemplating. The willow across the palm was torture enough but the leather strap weighted with lead across the backside was considered worse because of the humiliation of having to receive the punishment stripped from the waist down. Lesser violations were treated spontaneously with a smack across the jowls or a swift backhander. It was, preached Kavanagh, the best way of toughening them up, of preparing them for life in the outside world, a life spent staring at the coalface in Ballingarry or riveting in the shipyards of Cork.

Four weeks passed and Kavanagh, begrudgingly, admitted defeat. Cabrera was worth his weight in gold. The Spaniard was unlike any other teacher, or resident, of Innishannon. 'El Diablo', as he became known, was the first man they'd ever seen to have shoulder length hair, a goatee beard and skin that wasn't as white as the driven snow. He didn't shout, he talked, he didn't demand, he asked, and the boys, enamoured by his strange accent, hung on his every word.

Spanish lessons were not an official part of the curriculum, they were impromptu affairs, conducted only when the headmaster was out of earshot. The boys would listen, captivated, while he regaled stories of rural Andalucia and imparted words of advice, words which strengthened their resolve until they were old enough to leave.

'Repeat after me: Only a weak man will use his fists.'
'*Sólo un hombre débil utilizará sus puños.*'
'There is strength in silence.'
'*Hay fuerza en el silencio.*'
'Show not your pain but your courage.'
'*No mostrar dolor, mostrar coraje.*'

* * *

Callum and Cabrera sat silently as Father Leo, swathed in a ground-skimming cassock, belted at the waist,

49

welcomed the new recruit. In what appeared to be a dazzling display of schizophrenia, he tousled the young boy's hair, offered his mother tea and biscuits and reassured her that she had absolutely nothing to worry about. Saint Jerome's was a bastion of respectability with an impeccable reputation and a standard of teaching envied by many a school. The young lad had his doubts. Aged nine and a bit, he was neither unteachable nor an imbecile. He didn't know why he was there, or where his father had gone. Worse still, he'd heard of Saint Jerome's from the boys on the outside, he'd listened to tales of beatings and starvation. It filled him with dread. Cabrera caught his eye and, for a fleeting moment, he relaxed. It would be alright. The boy's mother made her excuses, thanked the headmaster and left. Abruptly. She didn't look back, nor did she say goodbye, she simply left and Father Leo's jolly disposition went with her. Brother Callum stood to leave and beckoned Cabrera to follow.

'We've lessons to do, best leave him to it,' he muttered. 'Trust me, it's for the best.'

Father Leo hovered behind the nervous new intake, leaned forward and whispered softly in his ear.

'Remind me now, what was your name?' he asked.

The young boy, sitting on his hands, smiled gently.

'Kieran,' he said.

The smack across the ear was hard enough to knock him off his seat.

'Kieran, *sir!*' yelled Kavanagh. 'Stand up!'

Petrified, the youngster rose to his feet and stood quivering before the headmaster, head bowed, hands clasped tightly behind his back.

'Where's your father?' asked Kavanagh, menacingly.

'Don't know, sir,' whispered Kieran.

'You don't know. You don't know because you haven't got one, and that makes you a bastard! What does it make you?'

'I'm not!' said Kieran, 'I do have a father, he's just…'

'Shut up! I can see you need a lesson in manners, boy!' boomed Kavanagh. 'Look at you, you're filthy, a disgrace. Are you not familiar with the phrase, 'Cleanliness is next to Godliness'? Well, by God, in this school, you will be clean, boy. Come with me.'

Father Leo frogmarched Kieran to the washrooms, forced him to strip and turned the shower on full blast. There was no hot water. Kieran scrubbed himself raw, terrified by what may follow. The water stopped. He shivered uncontrollably as a cold draught blew through the open windows. Kavanagh, grinning, tossed him a towel made of sandpaper, ordered him to dress and led him to the kitchens. Cockroaches scuttled across the floor, pans encrusted with burnt porridge sat on the cooker, discarded breakfast bowls lay in the sink. There was to be no education, no food and no privileges until he'd earned the right to receive them. Father Leo returned three hours later as Kieran was wiping down the worktop. The floor had been mopped clean, rows of spotless bowls were stacked neatly on the shelves and the pots on the stove gleamed like new. Leo inspected his handiwork and smiled.

'Well done, not bad for a first attempt,' he said, before slapping the boy across the face. 'Now do it again.'

* * *

Brother Callum said nothing. The boy was weak with hunger, his eyes heavy with exhaustion. He carried him to the dormitory in the garret and showed him to his bed, number 18 of 40. Before turning the mattress and dressing it in clean sheets, he gave the boy a couple of biscuits and apologised for the fact that his pockets couldn't hold more. By the time the other pupils clambered to their beds, Kieran was fast asleep.

Cabrera was on night watch. He crept silently up the stairs, paused outside the door, and listened. Using just his middle finger, he inched it open. Two boys, playing cards by the window, froze in fear as the darkened figure entered the dorm. He held a finger to his lips and winked. With a sigh of relief, the boys smiled and continued their game. The new boy was sleeping on his side. Cabrera walked around the bed and knelt beside him. The moonlight bathed his swollen, purple cheeks in a soft, blue light. His eyes, puffy and yellow, had all but closed up and a crimson scab was drying across the split on his lower lip.

* * *

'I'll thank you to keep your place Cabrera and remember who you're talking to!' shouted Father Leo 'You are not in charge here, I am the law and I will be obeyed. Do I make myself clear?'

A despondent Brother Callum cringed as he sat, head in his hands. There was no need to visit the dormitory, he'd seen it all before, he'd witnessed the abuse first hand and he'd even received a right hook on the one occasion he'd tried to intervene.

'Besides, I barely touched the lad,' said Kavanagh, defensively. 'A slap. That's all it was, a little slap.'

Cabrera said nothing. Armed with a bottle of iodine and a fistful of cotton wool, he returned to the dorm and gently rolled Kieran onto his back. His face was flawless.

* * *

The sky grew ominously dark. Dense clouds rolled in from the west, bringing with them the threat of another deluge. Brother Callum stood beneath the porch, arms folded, and looked out across the field, watching the hares run for cover.

'You're back then,' said Cabrera.

'Would you look at that sky,' said Callum. 'You'd think the devil himself was paying us a visit.'

'I think he's here already,' said Cabrera. 'I was wondering where you'd gone.'

'Had something to do.'

'Have you spoken to Leo about using the land for farming, growing vegetables?'

'I have indeed,' said Callum. 'And he'll have nothing to do with it.'

'Why not? It's a great idea.'

'That, is something only he and the good Lord can tell you, because I haven't a feckin' clue.'

Cabrera noticed a small, leather valise by his feet.

'Are you going away?' asked Cabrera.

Callum turned to face him.

'I am. Not far, but yes, I am going away. I'm leaving.'

'What?' said Cabrera, startled. 'Leaving? But why? Because of the vege…?'

'No, Constantine, not just that. I've had enough. I went to see if I could get a transfer but there's nothing available.'

'A transfer? But, what about…'

'I can't take it any more, Constantine. I cannot stand by and bear witness to Leo's abhorrent behaviour any longer. Especially that Kieran lad, he has it in for him.'

'I've noticed that too. He's normally quite fair when it comes to doling out the punishment but that poor boy does seem to bear the brunt of it.'

Callum shrugged his shoulders and sighed.

'You know, Constantine, I'd report it if I thought it'd make a difference, but it's like beating your head against a brick wall, and now my head hurts. I'm away.'

'Where will you go?' asked Cabrera.

'Not far. I've rented a house, just over the way there. I'll be able to keep an eye on you, so I will.'

* * *

Callum's departure had left a void. He'd been gone just a couple of weeks but it seemed like years. For Cabrera, it was like losing a friend, for the boys it was like losing a favourite uncle, someone who would pat them on the head, give them a biscuit and tell them everything would be okay. He headed for the field, desperate for some green space and fresh air. As he crossed the yard, he heard Father Leo's infernal rhetoric emanating from the chapel. Cabrera shielded his eyes from the dazzling sun and managed to catch just a fleeting glimpse of one of the pupils scurrying from the latrines to the dining rooms. Though brief, he recognised him instantly and gave chase.

'Kieran!' he said in loud whisper as he entered the canteen. 'Kieran, why aren't you in mass? You know Father Leo will be…' The door to the kitchen swung lazily on its hinges. Cabrera approached and slowly pushed it open with the back of his hand. There was no-one there. His eyes widened and his heart began to race. Tiny beads of perspiration gathered on his forehead.

'¿Qué quieres?' he shouted at the ceiling '*What do you want from me?*'

As usual, the boys polished off every morsel of their meagre supper and, though the night was drawing in, made the most of what little free time they had by playing in the yard. Cabrera watched from the window, saddened by the sight below. Unlike the children in Saleres, there was no laughter, no shouting or screaming, no elation or enthusiasm. It was as though every boy had had the child beaten out of them, they were fearful even of smiling. He watched as Father Leo circled the yard like a hawk eyeing its prey, when suddenly, he swooped. Of all the boys in the yard, only one was not running or jumping or kicking a ball. Only one stood motionless, hands in pockets, back to the wall. Keiran didn't see it coming. The palm of the hand slammed across his cheek and knocked him off balance. The headmaster yelled in his ear and gesticulated towards the other boys, obviously keen to know why he wasn't joining in. Cabrera ran from the office when he saw Leo grab him by the ear and drag him across the yard.

'Go about your business, Father Cabrera, this matter does not concern you.'

'It concerns me, Father Leo, when I see a boy chastised for no good reason.'

'I will not tolerate insolence in this school, Father Cabrera, not from the pupils and certainly not from you, now, be gone!'

* * *

Cabrera, hands behind his back, trod carefully as he moved between the rows of beds, fearful of waking the boys. They were all sound asleep, all save one, the boy in number 18, who was missing. Cabrera bit his lip, swore under his breath and ran downstairs, desperate to find him before Father Leo. The external doors were bolted from the inside, bar one, which led to the yard. Relieved he couldn't have gone far, he checked the latrines first, then made his way to the dining hall. The door was ajar. He waited as his eyes adjusted to the gloom then crouched to check beneath the tables.

'Kieran,' he whispered. 'It is Father Cabrera, everything is alright, you don't have to hide. Kieran, you can come out now.'

The only response was the sound of the wall clock, tick-tocking, echoing in the darkness. Just the kitchen remained. Anxious not to make a sound, he gently pushed the door open and peered inside.

'Kieran!' he gasped, alarmed at the sight of the boy heaped on the floor 'Kieran, ¿que está mal?'

The boy was unrecognisable, his face was a tender, swollen, puffy mound of rainbow-coloured bruises, a bone-deep gash across his cheek linked his pulverised nose to his bleeding ear, his lips, cracked and split, were turning blue and his right arm, broken at the shoulder and the wrist, was bent back behind his head. Cabrera took his hand and prayed. There was no pulse. He swallowed hard and suppressed his tears as his heart thumped with rage. Never before had he felt such anger, such hatred. Never before had he witnessed such barbaric brutality.

* * *

Father Leo picked himself up and rubbed his chin as if to soothe it.

'So, you fancy your chances, do you Constantine? Never had you down as pugilist.'

'This time you have gone too far!' snarled Cabrera. 'I will not stand by and watch it any longer. You must seek help or I will inform the authorities.'

'The authorities? And what exactly will you tell...'

'Enough! You have killed a boy, Leo! I have seen him! You are guilty of murder!'

'Murder?' said Leo, chuckling to himself, 'I've done no such...'

Cabrera grabbed him by the collar.

'I will remind you of your crime,' he hissed through gritted teeth, 'come with me!'

Kavanagh struggled to free himself as Cabrera hauled him from the office, dragged him across the yard and pushed him viciously through the kitchen door.

'Now do you remember, Leo!' he screamed. 'Now, do you...'

The kitchen was empty. No body, no blood, no stains. Cabrera stood wide-eyed, his hands trembling. Kavanagh shook his head and smirked, took him gently by the arm and guided him back to the office. He refused to drink the brandy, instead he sat, blinking rapidly, his neck twitching. Kavanagh studied him for a moment and made a phone call.

It didn't take long for the doctor to arrive. He waved his hand in front of Cabrera, shone a penlight into his eyes and tutted at the total lack of reaction. Cabrera did little to resist as the strait jacket was fastened behind his back. His vacuous eyes stared blankly into space.

'He'll be fine now he's sedated. Been seeing things, you say?'

'That's right doctor,' said Kavanagh. 'I'll not trouble you with the detail just now, suffice to say, it involved people who had, *passed*.'

'It's not uncommon. Probably stress, it can *unhinge* people.'

'It can that,' said Father Leo. 'It's a fragile thing, the human mind, it can snap, just like that. Where will you take him?'

'Carlow,' said the doctor. 'They know how to handle folk like, well, you know, like this.'

'Will he get better?' asked Leo.

'It's hard to say, but given time, and the right treatment, I dare say he'll be fine in a month or two.'

'A month or two? Are you sure that's long enough?'

The doctor placed the envelope in his jacket pocket, bid farewell to Kavanagh with a wink and secured Cabrera in the back seat. The rain drummed against the roof as they sped along the dark, deserted streets, slowing only for the usual traffic on the Douglas Road. The wipers squeaked against the windscreen as they sat silently waiting for the queue to move on. Cabrera slowly raised his head and peered through the rain-lashed window as they paused by Saint Finbarr's Hospital. A tall, dark figure hurried by, a clergyman, drenched and leaning into the wind, one hand clutching the biretta on his head, the other, dragging a small child who struggled to keep up.

* * *

The chapel fell silent. Still reeling from the departure of Brother Callum, the news that Father Cabrera had suddenly, and rather unexpectedly, returned to Spain left the boys in a state of shock. Without McGarvey or Cabrera, they were without an ally. A return to life under the headmaster's totalitarian dictatorship was not a regime change they looked forward too. The older boys voiced their disapproval, loud whispers at first which rapidly turned to chants, followed by hand clapping and the unified stamping of feet. Kavanagh's face, like the bulb on a thermometer, grew redder and redder as the rage boiled inside him. Then he snapped, unleashing a tirade of abuse as he stepped from the pulpit. Three of the older lads felt the wrath of his anger courtesy of a bible that smashed violently across their heads, bloodying their noses.

'You'll do well to remember where you are! There'll be no disquiet in a house of God!'

The crowd fell silent. The boys, fearful of catching his eye, studied their shoes, their fingernails and the floor. A slight boy seated towards the back of the chapel stood up and, ignoring the headmaster's demands that he return to his seat, fled. Kavanagh gave chase and cornered Kieran in the latrines. The young boy refused to cower, or beg forgiveness or even raise his arms in defence. An almighty slap across the cheek sent him flying to the floor. Unperturbed, blood trickling from his mouth, he scrambled to his feet, ducked by Kavanagh and ran to the kitchens. The windows above the sinks looked onto the field. From there, he could cross directly to Brother Callum's house, but, try as he might, the windows would not budge. He heard the door close behind him. Resigned to his fate, he climbed down and, in an act of defiance, raised his arms and offered up his chin. A right hook sent him spinning. His fragile jaw broke with the force of the punch. He lay, face down on the floor, almost, but not quite concussed, his frail body twitched with involuntary convulsions. Kavanagh knelt on his back, grabbed his arm by the wrist and wrenched it back until it cracked. Wracked with so much pain that he was unable even to scream, Kieran simply whimpered as his face was repeatedly smashed against the flagstones until it was nothing more than a bloody pulp. And then he was still. Kavanagh, panting, grinned and wiped the sweat from his brow.

* * *

It unnerved him. There was something odd about the whole scenario and it caused Callum McGarvey great unease. He hadn't seen Constantine in days and now, all of a sudden, every boy in the school was busy preparing the field for planting. For days, from sun up to sun down, they worked methodically in groups of six. The older boys systematically removed the turf, dug the soil over, forked it through and raked it to a fine till. Another group marked out the plots, 6ft x 3ft, and made drills in the soil. The younger boys were on their knees, gleefully sowing row upon row of carrots, turnips, cabbages, onions, potatoes and beetroot. Even odder still was the sight of Leo getting his hands dirty, intent on making a small patch of land his own. McGarvey watched suspiciously as he fervently stamped down the soil like a man possessed. It troubled him.

'Hope you're not burying your mistakes,' he muttered under his breath.

Chapter 6

'How many times have I told you, you can't just go taking stuff without asking,' said Maguire. 'It's against the law.'

'I risked my life getting these gardening gloves, Christ knows what disease I could've caught in that feckin' kitchen. Anyways, you're a fine one to talk so, you told me to steal the headmaster's shoes,' said O'Brien.

'And fancy footwear it is, too,' said Maguire. 'Have you sent them off, yet?'

'Not...'

'Do it now, and the gloves, before they realise they've gone. So, tell me, what did you make of him?'

'Who? McGarvey? He's alright,' said O'Brien, 'but I don't think it's him, he's too... weak, too nice, too old to go killing people. He'd do well to employ a cleaner though, the place is a feckin' health hazard.'

Maguire laughed.

'What's in the bag?' he asked. 'I've told you before, you can't afford to shop at Lidl.'

'Funny, so. It's my suit, dinner tonight – with Gráinne.'

'Why on earth do you need a suit to eat dinner?'

'It's her birthday. We've a table, at Flaherty's.'

'Flaherty's? Dear God, it must be serious, next thing you'll be wanting to marry her.'

'We are marr…'

The phone rang. O'Brien answered, listened for a second and hung up.

'Wrong number?' asked Maguire.

'That was Delaney. He sounded odd, he said we should go, now.'

'Get your coat.'

* * *

Delaney, somewhat flustered, met them on the steps by the main door.

'Thanks for coming, I wanted you to see this before we cleaned up.'

'Cleaned up?' said O'Brien 'What's happened? Has he…?'

'No, no, nothing like that. It may be nothing, might just be Cabrera outwardly exhibiting symptoms of some underlying trauma but, on the other hand, well, it might mean something to you.'

O'Brien looked anxiously at his boss.

'Mean something to us?' he whispered. 'Like what? I mean, he's been locked up for years, he doesn't even know Father Leo's dead.'

Maguire shrugged his shoulders. They followed Delaney down the long, dingy corridor and stopped outside the cell. Maguire peered through the window. Father Cabrera, it appeared, hadn't moved since their last visit. He was still seated in the same chair, still rocking back and forth, still smoking profusely. This time, however, he was completely naked and next to his blistered feet, amongst the cigarette butts, lay the fragments of a broken, plastic cup. Dried blood surrounded a shard protruding from a wound in his forearm.

'Has he tried to…' asked Maguire.

Delaney shook his head.

'No. He couldn't find a pen. I'm serious, look at the wall, right in front of him.'

Daubed in red, capital letters was a single word: 'ERUO'.

Maguire, saying nothing, stood aside and motioned his Sergeant to take a look.

'Eruo? What the feck does that mean?' said O'Brien.

'No idea,' said Delaney 'Thought you might know.'

'Is it an anagram, maybe?' said O'Brien.

'Sure, that's it,' said Maguire. 'He's trying to tell us to leave the Euro.'

'A whatsit then, you know, a word that stands for…'

'An acronym?' said Maguire. 'No, it's simpler than that. If that message is intended for us, there'll be nothing cryptic about it. Look it up, it's probably Spanish, or Portuguese, maybe.'

He turned to Delaney.

'Will he be alright?' he asked.

Delaney nodded.

'Sure, we'll get him cleaned up now, it's nothing serious. If anything happens, I'll let you know.'

Maguire glanced back at the writing on the wall.

'Doctor Delaney,' he said. 'Any chance I could take a look at those pictures? You know, the ones you said he did.'

Delaney's office was clinically white. White walls, white desk, white chair. He scanned a row of box files and pulled one down marked simply 'Cabrera'.

'Here you are,' he said. 'Not much to look at but he took some pleasure in it.'

Maguire flicked through the yellowing pages.

'Well, I don't think Picasso's got anything to worry about, that's for sure.'

O'Brien chuckled as he went through them.

'They're a bit odd,' he said, 'more like pictograms, arty pictograms. Look, a Chinaman, a man in a car, an aeroplane. He didn't even sign them!'

'What do the numbers mean? 7,6 and this one, 6,3?' asked Maguire.

'Can't help you there, I'm afraid,' said Delaney.

'Can I borrow these?'

'Of course.'

'Maybe get him an Etch-a-Sketch, eh?'

* * *

Back in the office, O'Brien sat wide-eyed, gazing at his laptop while Maguire, feet up, sipped a mug of tea.

'Have you not found it yet?' he asked impatiently.

'Nothing yet, but here's something interesting, 'cabrera' means 'place of goats'.'

'Why is that interesting?'

'I don't know.'

'Does he look like a goat?'

'No.'

'Does he smell like a goat?'

'No. Well, I presume he doesn't…'

'Well, then, why are you looking at goats instead of translating that word?'

'I am, I wasn't, I just thought… no, that's it, nothing. I give up. Do we not have some people that specialise in this kind of thing?' said O'Brien.

'We do. They're called Detective Sergeants. Keep looking.'

'I've looked. *Eruo* isn't Spanish or Portuguese or Italian, I don't know what else…'

'Well, it must be one of those feckin' latin languages, he doesn't speak anything else.'

O'Brien looked startled and smiled with delight.

'You, are a genius. I think. Hold on.'

'What've I said?' asked Maguire.

'Latin. Sure enough, there, see, it's Latin!'

'And that's why I'm a D.I. and you're a Sergeant. What's it mean?'

'Dig,' said O'Brien.

'Dig? For feck's sake, what does he mean, dig? Dig what? Dig where?'

O'Brien, flummoxed, leaned back and clasped his hands behind his head.

'I'm only a sergeant, how would I know?' he teased. 'Besides, don't forget, it might not even be for us, this *eruo* might be a message for Delaney.'

Maguire paced the room, holding his chin, whilst he pondered the suggestion.

'No. It's not for Delaney,' he said quietly.

O'Brien puffed out his cheeks, waiting for his boss to have a eureka moment.

'Maybe,' he said, 'maybe it's not the whole message.'

'What?' said Maguire, annoyed that his train of thought had been interrupted.

'Maybe he ran out of blood. Maybe he was trying to say 'can you dig it? like…'

'Will you hold your noise a moment!'

Maguire returned to his desk and stared at the sketches he'd borrowed from Delaney. He went through them one by one, then again, and again. A minute passed, then five, then twenty. He went to the bookshelf and pulled down a large volume entitled 'Chronicle of the Twentieth Century'. O'Brien Googled Flaherty's Restaurant and perused the menu in anticipation of his night out. He jumped as Maguire thumped his desk and gathered up the sketches.

'Look at this!' he said, holding up the first drawing. 'What do you see?'

O'Brien laughed.

'Oh, cartoon of a Chinaman.'

'And this?'

'Man in a car with his hair blowing in the wind.'

'And this?'

'A rocket, with a flower on the side.'

'Wrong! Wrong! Wrong!' yelled Maguire. 'Can you not see it? For Christ's sake, look again!' he said, his voice dropping to a whisper. 'Mao Tse-tung, died '76. Kennedy, shot, 1963. Apollo 1, blew up on the pad in 1967, and that aeroplane, over the mountains, Andes plane crash, '72.'

'What? I wasn't even born when half of those…'

'Remember what Brennan said? He had a sixth sense. He's telling us to dig.'

O'Brien grinned nervously.

'Are you sure?' he said 'I mean…'

'Think about it, Sergeant,' he said. 'Now, concentrate, what do you dig?'

'Stone Roses. No? Oh, I see, okay, the ground. You dig the ground,' said O'Brien, sitting up.

'Why?'

'To look for things, treasure, buried treasure, or, to plant things.'

'And what would you plant?'

'Flowers. Trees. Vegetables. *Vegetables*.'

'And where was Leo found?'

O'Brien chuckled.

'Oh, you have to admit, that is a bit far fetched, is it not?' he said, laughing, 'I mean, a mad priest who hasn't spoken for thirty years telling us to dig up a vegetable plot, it's like a Hollywood…'

Maguire clenched his teeth and glared at O'Brien.

'I'm on it,' said the sergeant, picking up the phone.

'Get the radar up there first,' said Maguire, 'we'll only dig if we find something.'

A Garda tapped the door, breezed in and handed Maguire a large, manilla envelope. He ripped it open and read the results from the lab. McGarvey's gloves harboured minute traces of black cotton, the same black cotton used to manufacture Father Leo's cassock. And there were hairs; four, short, silver-grey hairs which should have been in Leo's head.

O'Brien hung up.

'All set?' asked Maguire.

The Sergeant nodded.

'Aye, the fellas with the GPR will meet us there, anything else?'

'We'll need support, a Garda or two, at least. If we do have to dig, we'll have an audience faster than we can sell tickets. Oh, and here, read this.'

Maguire handed him the envelope.

'McGarvey's gloves came up trumps, we'll need a word, so we will.'

* * *

Father Brennan, flanked by a handful of sixth-formers, looked on excitedly as a bearded man in a hi-vis jacket and white hard hat trundled the GPR around the vegetable plot. His progress was painfully slow.

'Looks like a lawnmower!' he enthused.

'It's a GPR unit, Father,' said Maguire. 'Ground Penetrating Radar, it'll tell us if there's anything down there that shouldn't be, anything that's not a feckin' potato.'

'Like what, exactly, Inspector? What are you looking for?'

'Good question, I wish I knew myself.'

The man in the hi-vis hovered directly over the spot where Father Leo was found and stopped. A moment or two later, he reversed up, went forward and stopped again. He motioned to Maguire to join him. Together they scrutinised the screen attached to the handlebars as the operator pointed out anomalies beneath the surface.

'It's hard to tell,' he said, 'might be nothing, but I'd say it's worth a look.'

Maguire called O'Brien over.

'Call forensics and get a tent over this now,' he said. 'I want this sorted before we lose the light.'

Maguire gestured towards the house.

'I'm afraid this place is out of bounds till further notice, Father,' he said.

'What have they found?'

'Wouldn't like to say, but I'll keep you informed. You best go inside now.'

Slowly, gently, gradually, they removed the soil to a depth of three feet and stopped. A figure in a white boiler suit, paintbrush in hand, lay on the ground and leaned in. Moments later he gave Maguire a muddy thumbs up.

O'Brien sidled over, hands in pockets, grinning.

'It's like being on Time Team, so it is.'

'I'd stop grinning if I were you, you're having dinner with me tonight.'

'What?'

'We're off to see McGarvey, by the time we get back, this lot will have unearthed a puzzle for us. Might be a long night.'

'But Gráinne'll go mad!'

'Let there be no panic, she's a young lass, plenty more birthdays, so. Come on, you can call her on the way.'

* * *

Had he known the reason for their visit, Brother Callum may not have welcomed them so enthusiastically. He eased his ageing body into the armchair and smiled. Maguire sat, uncomfortably, amongst the discarded newspapers and penicillin cultures growing in the coffee cups whilst O'Brien stood by the door, trying not to breath too hard.

'It's like this Brother, see now, we know you were in the field that night, we know you were probably the last one to see Father Leo alive,' said Maguire.

'That's a hell of an accusation, Inspector! I've told you before I…'

'We have proof, Brother. Your…'

'Proof? What proof could you possibly have? You're… you're just trying to…'

McGarvey clutched his chest and wheezed uncontrollably, his right hand pointed towards the sideboard as his eyes threatened to pop from his head.

'The blue one,' he gasped, 'pass me…'

O'Brien snatched the inhaler and handed it to Callum. He drew deeply, two shots, and sank back in the chair. Maguire eyed O'Brien, his finger poised above the speed-dial on his phone. McGarvey relaxed.

'Sorry,' he said, sometimes it happens, if I…'

'Don't worry yourself. Will we come back?' asked Maguire.

'No, no, you're alright. Go on, where were we?'

Maguire paused until he was sure the old man was alright.

'Like I said, we have proof you were there that night, out in the field. Your gloves. They have traces of Leo's cassock on them, and some of his hair.'

McGarvey rubbed his head and grimaced as though he'd bitten a lemon.

'Alright! Alright, I saw him. But I didn't kill him, I couldn't kill any…'

'It's okay,' said O'Brien softly, 'we just need to know what you saw, it might help us. Take your time, just tell us what you saw.'

McGarvey gathered his thoughts and spoke quietly.

'It was late,' said Callum, 'past midnight. I was putting a stew on the hob and…'

'You were making a stew? At gone midnight?' asked Maguire.

'When else would I make it? I'm not a young man, Inspector, sleep does not come easy.'

'Go on.'

'I put the stew on the hob and went out back to get the veg, an onion, and maybe a turnip. When I got to the hedge, I stopped. I see these two fellas in the plot.'

'Two?' said Maguire.

'Right enough. Two. Looked like they were arguing or something. I stopped and waited. I watched to see what they were up to. Then one fella drops to his knees, I didn't know then that it was Leo, looked like he was digging, with his bare hands, like a dog. Then, he stopped, just like that, like he'd seen something, and he screamed.'

'Like he was in pain?' asked O'Brien.

'No, not really, it was more like a cry of… of despair.'

'And the other fella?'

'He ran away, back towards the school, I didn't see where.'

'So what did you do next?'

'I ran to help. If you can call it running. He was lying face down, dead, so he was. I knelt beside him to look at his face, that's when I saw it was Leo, he had this look, like he'd seen the devil himself. I stroked his hair and offered a prayer or two.'

'Then what?' asked Maguire.

'I reckoned I could do without the onion so I came back here, quick as I could. I don't mind admitting I was feeling, you know, a little, uneasy.'

'And the other man, did you get a look at him, could you describe him?'

'It was the middle of the night, Inspector, I could barely see my feet let alone some fella dressed in black,' said Callum.

'Black?'

'I think so.'

O'Brien's pocket warbled with the theme to 'Hawaii Five-O'. He stepped outside to take the call. Maguire leaned forward and spoke softly.

'Thing is, Brother,' he said, 'all the evidence we have points to you.'

Callum gasped.

'It's alright, I'm not going to arrest you, and, for what it's worth, I believe what you say is true, but I have to ask you to stay put, no going on holiday or taking a trip up the Nile or nothing, you're to stay right here, understand?'

'I understand, Inspector, I'll not be going anywhere.'

* * *

Maguire joined O'Brien outside and stared across the field.

'Well?' he asked. 'What did they want?'

'They found a shin bone, sir,' said O'Brien.

'A shin bone? Is that it?'

'Not quite. The shin bone's connected to a knee bone.'

'What?'

'And the knee bone's connected to a thigh bone.'

'I'll count to three.'

'Skeleton, intact, they're exhuming it now.'

Chapter 7

Maguire stabbed the noodles and raised a forkful of chicken chow mein to his mouth. O'Brien looked on with contempt as he shovelled it in. Flaherty's, it was not.

'Can you believe this?' he said, returning to the document. 'That skeleton has a fractured skull, a broken shoulder, a broken jaw and the arm is busted in two places. I'm surprised someone could do that to a kid.'

'Nothing surprises me anymore,' said Maguire, 'not even these prawn crackers. Someone knocked seven bells out of him, that's for sure, and whoever it was, was a big fella. Have they got any DNA off it yet?'

'Later,' said O'Brien.

'Good, at least then we have a chance of finding out who the poor sod was. Right, I'm off to see that Father Brennan before he goes to bed, have a look at those school records, see if I can find something.'

'Right you are,' said O'Brien, 'will I get off then?'

'You will not get off, Sergeant, you will search the records for any kid that disappeared forty or fifty years ago. He'll be local, preferably the same height as the skeleton and a gardening enthusiast.'

'Sir.'

* * *

Despite the hour, Father Brennan was happy to help. He unlocked an old, glass-fronted cabinet and heaved the black, leather-bound registers onto his desk. They smelled musty and stale. Details of every pupil admitted to the school till 1965 were logged in an indigo, hand-written script across the foolscap pages. Name, age, date of birth, date of arrival, address (if any), parents (if any), guardian (if any), date of departure and whether employment was secured. The headmaster sat opposite Maguire and began skimming through the yellowed pages.

'And what exactly are we looking for, Inspector?' he asked enthusiastically.

'Well, Father, I'd be looking for an entry that says something like, I don't know, ran away, absconded, or gone missing, maybe.'

'Right you are! Will you take a drink, some ice cream, maybe?'

Maguire raised his eyes with a look of temptation.

'It's Ben and Jerry's. Chunky Monkey.'

Maguire declined.

'Best not,' he said. 'Sounds too much like Mrs Maguire. Tea will be fine.'

* * *

Two hours later Maguire slammed shut the final volume.

'Nothing, Father,' he moaned. 'I was convinced we'd find something. I'm sorry for taking up so much of your time. Doesn't look as though any of them got parole.'

'Think nothing of it, Inspector, the pleasure was mine. Actually, I found it quite interesting, I never realised how old these were till I saw some of the dates.'

Maguire twitched.

'Dates? Father, you can tell me to feck off if you like, but would you mind going through them again?'

'Again?'

'Yes, only this time, just look for an entry that doesn't have a date of departure, just a blank, it won't take long, I'm sure.'

Thirty minutes later, Maguire called O'Brien.

'You're looking for a kid called McCulloch,' he said. 'I'm not even sure he went missing but he's the only possible. You'll have to go back forty years so, maybe more. We've an address on Claregate Street. See what you can find.'

* * *

O'Brien, slumped across his keyboard, woke with a start as Maguire slammed four bottles of Murphy's on the desk.

'Here's your prize for staying awake,' he said.

'Thanks, thanks very much!' said O'Brien, reaching for the bottle opener.

'And give this to Gráinne, with my apologies.'

'Chocolates? You didn't have to…'

'I know, I'm all heart. So, how'd you get on? Did you find a McCulloch?'

O'Brien opened the bottles, passed one to Maguire and took a swig from his.

'Yes and no. There's no record of any kid by that name going missing but I did find a McCulloch. The only McCulloch in the whole parish and she's lived here all her life. I'm assuming, I'm hoping, she's the one we're looking for.'

'You mean she's still breathing?'

'Indeed she is. Miss Maureen McCulloch.'

'Feckin' grand, at last, something… hold on, 'Miss'? Is she the sister maybe?'

'Nope, too old, she would have to be the mother. She's still there, though, on Claregate Street. Number 9.'

Maguire perched on his desk and knocked back the stout.

'Well, if it is her kid,' he said, 'and she is a "miss", that means she never married, had the baby out of wedlock. Jesus, it's a wonder she didn't end up in Carlow.'

'Can't have been easy,' said O'Brien. 'She must've been the talk of town.'

'Right, so. We'll have a chat, tomorrow, not too early, wouldn't want to wake the old dear. Good work there, Sergeant. Anything else?'

'Yes. You'll like this. Those diaries we borrowed, I had a look through them and…'

'Have you no manners? You do know it's rude to read someone else's diary, don't you?' said Maguire with a smirk. 'They write all kinds of personal things in there, the kind of things you wouldn't want to know about.'

'How do you know?' asked O'Brien.

'Herself has one. Reads like the feckin' Exorcist, so it does. So, come on, what was it then? Did he fancy the Bishop? Unrequited love, that sort of thing?'

'Not that interesting I'm afraid.'

'Well, what did he write?' asked Maguire.

'It's not what he wrote, it's what the G.P. wrote. Found this.'

O'Brien held up a prescription from Kavanagh's doctor and handed it to his boss.

'This is only a few weeks old,' said Maguire. 'What the feck is 'Risperidone'?'

'I looked it up. It's an anti-psychotic drug,' said O'Brien, 'stops you hallucinating, that kind of thing.'

'Hallucinating? He wasn't psychotic, was he?'

'I don't think so, but here's the thing. They also give it to people with Alzheimer's.'

'Alzheimer's? Leo had Alzheimer's?' said Maguire.

'Maybe. I mean, there's a good chance, I think.'

'I think so too. You know what else this means, don't you? It means old Father Brennan would've known about it. Withholding information, serious offence, so it is.'

'That's not all, I found these pressed between the pages,' said O'Brien, holding up a sweet wrapper.

Maguire was overwhelmed with nostalgia.

Big Time toffee bar!' he exclaimed. 'Not seen that since I was a kid, guaranteed to break your teeth, so it is, and Sweet Afton's, Christ we used to smoke those thinking we were posh! Ah, well, so he saved a few things, like a scrapbook, so...'

'I don't think so,' said O'Brien. 'These were with them.'

He held up two sheets of paper, on one was written the address of the school and on the other, two words: 'Leo Kavanagh.' Maguire frowned.

'Look at this,' said O'Brien as he placed both sheets next to the page they'd retrieved from Father Kavanagh's pocket. The handwriting was identical.

'Whoever wrote 'Cabrera' wrote these as well.'

Maguire sighed heavily.

'Do me a favour,' he said. 'Father Brennan, run a check on him, see what comes up.'

O'Brien looked surprised.

'A check?' he said. 'On Father Brennan?'

'Nothing wrong with your hearing, is there?'

'I know, but, a priest?'

'Never judge a book by its cover, Sergeant. Something's giving me indigestion and it's not the stout.'

Chapter 8

'Don't trouble yourself, Miss McCulloch, really, we're fine,' said Maguire.

'It's no trouble, Inspector, I don't mind. I'll put the kettle on, just give me a minute, and the name's Maureen.'

Maureen McCulloch hadn't changed much since her youth. Back then, she would've been called a 'frail', slight of build, no more than seven stone and peaking at five feet two inches in height. Her hair, now grey, was short and neat; her eyes, emerald green, still sparkled.

Maguire glanced around the house. It was not unlike his own, apart from the fact hers was stuck in 1957. Furnishings were sparse, bordering on the basic. There were no pictures on the wall, no family photos, no ornaments. Just a mirror above the fireplace and a large, wooden crucifix leaning on the mantelpiece. A three-bar electric heater stood on the hearth. O'Brien squeezed next to Maguire on the tiny sofa.

'Here we are,' she said, returning from the kitchen. 'I've no biscuits but I can do you a slice of bread and butter if you like.'

'Tea's grand, Maureen, just grand, thanks, so,' said Maguire.

'Well, how can I help?' asked Miss McCulloch. 'If it's about the neighbours, I can't...'

'It's not about the neighbours, Maureen, I'm afraid it's a bit more sensitive than that. We were wondering, did you ever, er, did you ever have any children? A son, maybe?'

Miss McCulloch took a deep breath and nodded.

'I did. But...'

'It's alright, Maureen, I don't want to upset you, it's just a few questions, that's all. In fact, you don't have to answer anything if you don't want to, we can leave right now if you'd prefer.'

'I don't mind, Inspector. Ask away.'

Maguire cleared his throat.

'Well, first of all, just so we're clear, was your boy at St. Jerome's?' he asked.

Miss McCulloch sighed remorsefully.

'That place was like a prison, so it was,' she said. 'I didn't want to do it, I didn't want to send him there but I had no choice. It wasn't the proudest moment of my life.'

Maguire hesitated.

'If you don't mind me... you weren't married, were you?'

'No, Inspector. I was not. Life wasn't easy being a single parent back then.'

'I understand.'

'It wasn't just that I couldn't cope. It was the abuse as well. I couldn't take it.'

'The abuse?'

'The name calling. Being shouted at in the street. Being spat upon.'

'What about the father, Maureen, did he not want to, I mean…'

'The father wouldn't, or should I say, couldn't, do anything about it,' she replied. 'He had his fun and that was that. Truth be known, I was too scared, I suppose.'

'Too scared?' asked O'Brien. 'What do you mean, Miss McCulloch, too scared? Too scared to… what?'

'To speak up, tell anyone what happened. They would never have believed me.'

'I might believe you, if you want to tell me, that is,' said O'Brien, softly.

Maureen pulled her cardigan tight around her chest, folded her arms and took a deep breath.

'He was, shall we say, a respectable man. A pillar of the community. That's why I kept quiet. The thing is, he forced himself upon me, Sergeant. He took advantage. I was young, I wasn't strong enough to… it's the only time I've ever been, *intimate*, with a man.'

O'Brien paused before continuing.

'You mean, he raped you?' he asked quietly.

'He did that. I was fifteen years old.'

'Fifteen? And you're sure he was the father?'

'As I said, it's the only time I've ever… I'm absolutely certain.'

Maguire rubbed his forehead, leaned forward and spoke softly.

'I am so sorry, Maureen,' he said, eyes full of compassion. 'Really, I am. Have you any idea what became of the boy?'

'He ran away, that's what the school told me, he ran away on his tenth birthday. You'd have thought he'd have run back here, but no, he didn't.'

'Did they search for him?'

'Apparently. Not very hard if you ask me. I gave up hope after a year. Gave up waiting for that knock at the door,' she paused and frowned at Maguire. 'Why?' she continued, 'are you telling me you've found him?'

'Well, I don't want to upset you but we have found, we've found a body. We think it might be him.'

'God rest his soul, if it is. How will you know?'

'It's called a DNA test.'

* * *

It was early. Maguire was grinding his teeth out of sheer frustration. Brother Callum McGarvey was giving him cause for concern. He wanted to believe his innocence but with no other suspects there was simply no other feasible line of inquiry, even if all the evidence was circumstantial. For over an hour he'd been trying to establish a feasible motive for killing Father Kavanagh but he could find none. O'Brien, he concluded, was right. McGarvey didn't fit the bill, but something bugged him, like an insatiable itch. The bit about the two fellas in the field. It wasn't implausible but it didn't add up. Unless McGarvey was on Risperidone too, someone wasn't telling the whole truth.

O'Brien breezed through the door and tossed Maguire a greasy, white paper bag.

'Bacon, brown sauce, toasted,' he said, grinning.

'What are you so happy about?' asked Maguire.

'Gráinne loved the chocolates.'

'That's it?'

'I mean, *she loved* the chocolates,' said O'Brien, with a wink.

'Oh, I get it, or rather you did. Well, don't thank me, thank Lily O'Brien. I only saved you a fortune at Flaherty's. You owe me.'

'I do that.'

'What's that there?' asked Maguire. 'Doesn't look like bird seed.'

'It's not. Tis a tasty sausage, egg and crispy bacon in a lovely, white bap.'

'Sounds like you had an energetic night, don't make a habit of it or you'll end up with a belly like mine. Best contraceptive in the world, so it is. Did you run a check on our friend Father Brennan?'

'I did so. Now, here's the thing, he's everywhere you'd expect him to be, electoral register, RSA, that kind of thing, and, there's tons about him as a priest, since leaving the seminary to becoming Head at Saint Jerome's, but...'

'But what?' screeched Maguire, brown sauce dripping down his chin. 'Don't keep me in suspense.'

O'Brien grinned.

'But there's no record of him with Births, Marriages and Deaths.'

'What? Are you feckin' sure?'

'Sure as I'll ever be.'

'Did you spell it right?'

'I did that. Even Saint Finbarr's don't have a record of him. Believe it or not, there have only ever been four Brennans registered here in the last eighty years and they're all dead.'

'I'm beginning to wish this one was.'

Maguire devoured his sandwich in silence and wiped his chin.

'Put it on the list. Looks like old Father Brennan has some serious explaining to do. By the way, there's a package on your desk, from the lab I think. Way things are going, it's bound to be bad news.'

O'Brien sat down and ripped open the envelope.

'It's not as bad as you think,' he said.

'How so?'

O'Brien smiled.

'We've got a match,' he said. 'Miss McCulloch. It's her boy alright.'

'Well, that's something,' said Maguire, 'at least now we know who he…'

'Hold on,' said O'Brien, turning over the page. 'Holy feckin' shite! We've got another one, too.'

'What? Another match?'

'Yes. Now we know who the father is.'

'What? Who?'

'Leo Kavanagh.'

* * *

The clock on the mantelpiece chimed the hour. One o'clock in the morning. Callum shuffled to the kitchen, unwrapped the pork chop and gave it a sniff. It was, perhaps, past its best, but it wasn't moving and he didn't keel over. He laid it in the pan, atop the blackened debris from previous stove-top pursuits and doused it with vegetable oil. The gas burner burst into life, devouring the match and blistering his fingertips. The meat sizzled as the oil, spitting and hissing, grew hotter and hotter. The plate from last night's repast was barely scarred. He gave it a wipe with a decaying sponge, set it to one side and opened a small tin of peas. Ten minutes and it would be charred to a cinder, long enough to annihilate anything bacterial that may, in time, turn his stomach. He flipped the chop, returned to his chair, and strained, by the light of the single bulb dangling from the ceiling, to read the racing results from The Curragh. Within minutes he was dozing.

Flames danced around the smouldering lump of pork as the oil ignited and rapidly carbonised everything in the pan. Callum coughed as smoke billowed from the kitchen, then he woke and began to choke as panic set in. With one hand over his mouth, he grabbed the pan from the hob and tossed it into the overcrowded sink. The steam and toxic smoke overwhelmed his throat, closing it till it was as good as sealed. He dropped to the floor, suffocating, and tried in vain to reach the inhaler on the sideboard.

* * *

Cabrera opened his eyes.

'Que en paz descanse,' he whispered. 'Rest in peace.'

Chapter 9

'I found this, Inspector, thought it might help you.'

'I'm afraid it's a bit late for photographs, Maureen, shall we sit down?'

O'Brien stood by the door as Maguire took a seat opposite Miss McCulloch. He rubbed his hands and stared, momentarily at the carpet. His words were soft and slow.

'Do you remember how we took a wee sample from your cheek, Maureen, for the DNA test I explained to you? How we could use it to see if it matched the body we found?'

'I do, Inspector, and did it? Did it match?'

'It did. I'm sorry to say the body we found is your son, Keiran.'

Miss McCulloch closed her eyes and crossed herself.

'Thank you, Inspector,' she said. 'Thank you, very much.'

'We'll make sure he gets a decent burial, Maureen, you can be sure of that. At least now he can rest in peace.'

'Can you tell me, where, where did you find him?'

'Er, not far, near the school. I'm afraid he was very young when he passed.'

Miss McCulloch nodded knowingly at the Inspector.

'About ten I'd say.'

Maguire looked surprised.

'Yes,' he said 'About 10.'

'How did he... do you know how he died?'

'Well,' said O'Brien, 'it looks as though he was...'

Maguire interrupted.

'*That*, is something we may never know. I'm sorry,' he said. 'Look, there's something else. Something I feel obliged to tell you.'

'Go on, Inspector, I'm too old to be shocked,' said McCulloch.

'We found,' he paused, 'in the course of our inquiries, we found *another* match for the boy's remains. What I mean is, we know, *we know* who the father is.'

Miss McCulloch turned as white as a sheet.

'What?' she gasped, holding her hand to her face as her eyes welled up 'Oh, sweet Lord, the shame of it. How can you? I...'

'There's nothing to be ashamed of, Maureen, you've done nothing wrong,' said Maguire reassuringly. 'It was Leo Kavanagh who committed the crime, it was he who abused his position. You're the innocent in this. Listen, I know it's not much comfort, but you might like to know, he's passed away too.'

Miss McCulloch heaved herself from the chair.

'I think we need a cup of tea,' she said. 'I'm so embarrassed, give me a moment.'

O'Brien looked at Maguire and raised his eyebrows.

'Sorry, sir,' he said. 'Almost...'

'Don't worry yourself, it's never easy, breaking news like that. Sometimes you just have to, well, you know.'

Miss McCulloch returned with a pot and three cups. Maguire picked up the photograph and smiled. The blurry black and white snap showed two mischievous looking boys in short trousers with pudding bowl haircuts sitting next to each other, arms aloft, laughing.

'How old was he here?' he asked.

'About six, I think. It was taken outside, on the wall,' said Miss McCulloch.

'They look alike, must've been great mates.'

'They were, Inspector, but they weren't just friends. That's his brother.'

'Brother?' asked Maguire.

'I had twins,' said Miss McCulloch.

'Twins?' said Maguire, turning to face O'Brien 'What, what happened to the other...'

'He fell ill, not long after that photo was taken, I think. I thought it was just a cold at first but it got worse. Much worse. I didn't know what to do. His father, you know, *him*, he took him to Saint Finbarr's. That was the last I saw of him. They said it was TB.'

'TB?' said Maguire.

'He passed soon afterwards. There was nothing they could do. My only regret is I didn't even have the chance to say goodbye.'

'But what about the burial? Surely then you...'

'Father Kavanagh took care of it. It all happened so quickly. He made it quite clear that, because of my, *situation*, there could be no headstone. He's in a pauper's grave somewhere, but I couldn't tell you where,' said McCulloch.

'And Kavanagh?'

'I never saw him again.'

* * *

A light drizzle peppered the windscreen as they drove the twenty minutes from Claregate Street to the school. O'Brien, ignoring the frown carved deep into Maguire's forehead, broke the silence.

'Are you okay?' he asked. 'You seem a bit stressed.'

'A bit stressed?' said Maguire. 'We found a feckin' priest face down in the onions, then a skeleton we weren't looking for, we find out who it is but not who put him there and we still don't know who killed that shite Kavanagh. Way things are looking I wouldn't be surprised if it was Colonel feckin' Mustard with the candlestick.'

O'Brien's phone rang.

'And if that's Steve McGarrett, tell him to feck off, I'm busy.'

* * *

Father Brennan, somewhat surprised, rose from behind his desk and greeted them with outstretched arms. Maguire declined the offer of tea and instead, patience wearing thin, remained standing and scowled at the headmaster.

'This looks serious, Inspector, best tell me how can I help.'

'Well, you see Father, I won't beat around the bush, it's like this. I know you're a man of the cloth and all, so I'm not going to accuse you of lying. Let's just say you weren't telling us the whole truth. How's that with you?'

'I'm not sure what you mean, Inspector, not telling you the whole truth about…'

'You'll remember, no doubt, I asked you if you'd noticed anything odd about Father Leo's behaviour before he passed and you said no.'

'Did I? Well, then, that must be true,' said Father Brennan.

'Not getting a touch of the old Alzheimer's, there, are you, Father?' asked Maguire.

'I'm sorry? I…'

'Risperidone.'

'Ah.'

Father Brennan sat down and poured himself a tumbler of water.

'So, the Risperidone,' said Maguire. 'He wasn't psychotic, was he?'

'No. No, Father Leo wasn't psychotic, he was suffering with dementia. Just over a year now.'

'Bad?' asked O'Brien.

'He had his moments,' said Father Brennan, 'the thing is, they were beginning to happen with alarming regularity. One day he was as lucid as ever and others, well, he didn't have a clue basically, about anything. About where he was, what he was doing, what he should eat, what he should wear. It's a terrible thing to behold, Inspector. Terrible.'

'So, tell me,' said Maguire, 'if the doctor prescribed the drugs, why wasn't he taking them?'

Father Brennan sipped from the glass.

'Not taking them?' he said.

Maguire scratched the back of his head and pulled a piece of paper from his pocket.

'This prescription is seven weeks old,' he snarled.

'Right so,' said Father Brennan with a look of resignation. 'We tried, Inspector, believe me, we tried keeping up the medication. Sometimes he'd take it, other times he'd spit it out. The funny thing was, if he was compos mentis, he'd have nothing to do with them.'

The headmaster watched in silence as Maguire, arms folded, slowly paced the room.

'Tell me,' he said, 'people with Alzheimer's, they have a tendency to go a wandering, do they not?'

Father Brennan smiled.

'That, they do, Inspector, that they do. Many's the time I've had to chase after Leo and bring him back.'

'I can believe that,' said Maguire with a chuckle. 'My granny succumbed to the old dementia too, we'd find her a half a mile away, not a care in the world.'

Maguire gazed from the window onto the yard below, his back to the headmaster.

'I'm guessing you had to chase after Leo the night he died,' he said, slowly raising his voice. 'I'm guessing you were out there in the field with him. I'm guessing you were with him when he…'

'Yes! Alright, I was there,' said Father Brennan. 'I was there, I was with him!'

'That'll be the correct answer,' said Maguire. 'Here, won't need to embarrass you with these now.'

'My shoes! I was wondering… where did …did you steal…?'

'Borrowed, Father Brennan. We borrowed them. Sign this please, just to say you got them back safe and sound, and put the address too.'

Maguire handed O'Brien the receipt.

'Perfect match, so they are.'

'Match?'

'Your shoes, to the prints we found in the allotment. We knew Leo wasn't alone when he died and your man, Callum, confirmed it.'

Maguire turned to O'Brien and gave him a wry smile.

'God bless Callum McGarvey,' he said.

'Indeed,' said the headmaster, crossing himself. 'God bless Callum McGarvey.'

Maguire looked confused.

'What do you mean?' he asked.

'You haven't heard?'

'Obviously not.'

'Brother Callum, he died last night. They found him this morning.'

'What? How? What happened?' asked Maguire.

'There was a small fire apparently, in the kitchen. They said he died from smoke inhalation, well, an asthma attack really, brought on by the smoke,' said Father Brennan. 'I believe the term they used was asphyxiation.'

Maguire turned to O'Brien.

'Did you know about this?'

'News to me,' said O'Brien.

'This is turning out to be one hell of day,' said Maguire.

'It's not all bad,' said O'Brien 'Look.'

O'Brien held up the receipt in his left hand, in his right, the piece of paper from Kavanagh's diary with the school's address written on it.

'You wrote that, didn't you Father?' said Maguire. 'And you wrote 'Cabrera' on the note we pulled from Leo's…'

Father Brennan slumped in his chair and shook his head furiously.

'Yes, yes, yes! I wrote it!'

'I'm all ears,' said Maguire.

'I used them as memory aids. I used to sit with Leo whenever he took a turn for the worse and show him the pieces of paper, trying to jog his memory. His address, names of people he knew, I even... I even bought old chocolate bars and cigarette boxes off eBay to help him.'

'You're not all bad, Father.'

'What happens now?' asked Father Brennan. 'Am I under arrest?'

Maguire smirked.

'Don't tempt me. Now, back to the case in hand. The night Kavanagh died. Tell us exactly what happened and this time I want the truth, the whole truth and nothing but the truth.'

* * *

Kavanagh stood, arms unfurled, like some religious effigy rising from the mist and watched in boyish wonder as a doe and her fawn grazed across the field. The moon, now high, cast a pale, blue light across his wrinkled face. Slowly, he turned full circle, head upturned, absorbing everything that surrounded him, impervious to the cold, damp air, safe within his childhood. An owl took flight as a distant cry disturbed the peace. Father Brennan pleaded with him to return to the house. Kavanagh froze, suddenly unsure of his surroundings, fearful of the stranger who approached with alarming speed. Callum McGarvey crouched behind the hedgerow and watched as Father Leo lowered his arms in distress and begged the stranger to stay away. Father Brennan slowed to a casual walk and raised his arms in a gesture of surrender.

'It's alright, Leo, it's only me,' he said. 'Paddy Brennan. Will we go inside now?'

Leo, squinting, regarded him quizzically then, in a moment of recognition, winced in disbelief at the young boy strolling towards him. A small, frail boy aged nine and a bit.

'No! It cannot be!' he gasped, his face tortured by grief. 'It cannot be! I'll show you!'

He ran, as best he could, towards the vegetable plot, stumbling and cursing along the way. He checked over his shoulder and cried aloud as Father Brennan closed in on him. Panicking, he dropped to his knees and dug, frantically, with his bare hands, clawing at the soil, muttering and swearing under his breath, sweat trickling down his face.

'It cannot be! By the power of Christ, it cannot be!' he hissed.

Father Brennan leaned forward and placed a calming hand on his shoulder.

'It's alright Leo, don't be scared, come now, let's go inside,' he said.

Leo froze, his fragile heart stalled. Petrified, he turned his head and gasped for air. Father Brennan smiled, his face a battered, bloodied mess of multi-coloured bruises, his cheek split wide open, his eyes swollen shut.

Brother Callum looked on as a tall figure, clad in black, fled towards the house.

* * *

'And you left him there?' asked O'Brien sternly. 'You left him there and you didn't think to call for an ambulance, or the police even?'

'I panicked, Sergeant! I didn't know what to do, God forgive me, I feel bad enough as it is.'

O'Brien stepped forward and gazed down at the headmaster.

'Thing is,' he said. 'I don't think you do.'

Maguire reclined on the sofa, crossed his legs and eyed Father Brennan with a look of mistrust.

'Something else,' he said, 'and try to be honest, Father, that's why you wear the frock. Do you remember how old you were when you came to this school?'

Father Brennan, clearly embarrassed, cleared his throat and spoke quietly.

'I do. About six or seven, I think, give or take a year.'

'And before that. Do you recall anything about your family? Where you lived, for example? Your parents?' asked Maguire.

'Very little. As I said before, Inspector, I was orphaned. I was raised by a foster family.'

'And you have no idea what became of your real parents? Or why they gave you up?'

'None at all.'

Maguire blew out his cheeks and huffed, clearly unsettled by what he believed to be a charade.

'Thing is, Father,' he said, 'we have no record of you.'

'Well, I've never been in trouble with the police, Inspector.'

'I mean, before your arrival at Saint Jerome's. There is no record of anyone by your name on the register at Births, Marriages and Deaths, and no record of you at Saint Finbarr's either.'

Father Brennan anxiously rubbed the back of his neck and sighed.

'Well,' he said, 'it doesn't surprise me. I don't even have a birth certificate.'

O'Brien chipped in.

'Well, then, where do you suppose you got your name?' he asked.

'I suppose I got it from my foster family.'

'Wrong again, Father,' said Maguire. 'The only Brennans in the parish passed away childless or long before you came on the scene.'

'In that case, Inspector, you know as much as I do. I'm sorry I can't be more helpful.'

Maguire turned to O'Brien.

'Funny how the mind can hit delete when it wants to, eh, Sergeant? One last thing before we leave, Father,' he said as he stood to leave, 'that scratch on your cheek, that wasn't a rose was it? It was Leo Kavanagh.'

The headmaster touched his cheek.

'Yes,' he whispered. 'It was Leo.'

'We'll need a DNA sample. Nurse O'Brien, here, has a swab.'

Chapter 10

Each night, as the lights went out, an eerie stillness descended over the hospital. The receptionist, with only the internet for company, divided her time between the well-thumbed pages of OK! magazine and a smartphone as idle as herself. Behind her, tucked away in a cubbyhole of an office, dozed a security guard, oblivious to the bank of ever-changing images on the cctv screens, oblivious to the old lady standing in the corridor, the old lady who watched, entranced, as the naked, hunched figure of a man rocked rhythmically back and forth in his chair like a weary metronome. A plume of smoke, tinged by moonlight, streamed skyward from a burning butt laying on the floor whilst the well-worn rosary beads clicked as they slipped swiftly through his fingers. They stopped, abruptly, as she slowly raised a hand and placed it softly against the window. His shoulders sagged with the weight of his sigh. He stood, turned to face her and stepped lethargically from the shadows. His face, just inches from hers, was tormented by pain and wrinkled with grief. He placed his right hand opposite hers and breathed deeply. Her emerald green eyes seemed to lighten with relief.

* * *

A handful of cotton clouds drifted lazily across the sky. Maguire pulled a pair of sunglasses from his breast pocket.

'Give me the keys,' he said. 'I'll drive.'

O'Brien obliged.

'Why don't we just take your car?' he asked.

'Because, Mrs Maguire used it last night and it feckin' stinks.'

'Stinks, of what? Kebabs? Perfume?'

'Mrs Maguire does not use perfume, Sergeant, she uses Airwick.'

'Is that why you look so feckin' miserable?' asked O'Brien.

Maguire adjusted the seat and fastened his safety belt.

'I hate loose ends, Sergeant, I like my cases wrapped up like a Christmas present, nice and neat, sealed tight with a feckin' bow on the top.'

O'Brien grinned.

'You've a way with words, so you have,' he said, 'but tis only the bow that's missing. I mean, we know *how* Kavanagh died, we just don't what caused it. May well have been the cold.'

Maguire sneered as he fired the engine and sped towards Claregate Street.

'The cold?' he said.

'Right so, look, an old fella with a weak heart, outside at two in the morning in the freezing fog with only the Alzheimer's for company, what do you expect?'

'I suppose you're right,' said Maguire. 'I just keep thinking old Father Brennan... like, he's not letting on, like there's something...'

'No, can't see it myself. The only thing Father Brennan needs to do is go to confession.'

'Ha! Right so, better book himself in for an hour or two.'

'Plus a couple of hours for the old penance. He'll have sore knees by the time he's through,' said O'Brien. 'Anyways, you should be happy so, after all, we found that lad and laid him to rest, that's quite a result, you should be proud.'

Maguire relented with a sigh of exhaustion.

'I know, I know, but we still don't know who killed him.'

'Ah, come on, we both know who killed him, we just can't prove it,' said O'Brien.

'You're right, I should stop worrying,' said Maguire, 'probably just the Airwick going to my head. We should celebrate, in fact, I'll let you buy me a pint.'

'Very kind, thanks.'

'Of whiskey. Did you bring those DNA test results?' asked Maguire.

'I did. Right here. The old girl should be happy,' said O'Brien.

'Might be a bit of a shock for her. Hope you've got the de-fibs in the boot.'

Hawaii Five-O bellowed from O'Brien's coat pocket.

'Pull over,' he said.

'Don't tell me, it's Gráinne, she's booked you into the honeymoon suite at The Hilton.'

'Nope. It's Delaney.'

O'Brien listened intently, saying nothing. His face dropped as he terminated the call.

'It's Cabrera,' he mumbled. 'He passed away, about an hour ago.'

'What?' said Maguire. 'Not another one! How?'

'Natural causes, apparently. They found him laying on his bed, arms folded across his chest, holding his rosary, smiling almost, like he knew he was going to die.'

Maguire sucked his teeth as he tapped the steering wheel with his right hand.

'Remind me to call Inspector Barnaby when we get back,' he said, starting the engine.

'Barnaby?'

'Midsomer Murders. Fit right in, so he will.'

* * *

Maguire slowed as they entered Claregate Street, the road ahead was partially blocked.

'Don't like the look of this,' he said as they approached Miss McCulloch's house. An ambulance, doors ajar, straddled the kerb by the front door.

Maguire flashed his warrant card.

'Maureen McCulloch?' he asked.

'Afraid so,' said the medic. 'Thought you lot had been and gone.'

'We're a different lot,' said Maguire. 'How long?'

'About an hour ago.'

'Who called the ambulance?'

'Neighbour, she's inside if you want to see her. Drops by every morning with a pint and a paper. Called the police when she didn't get an answer, then we arrived.'

Maguire sighed.

'Anything, anything unusual?' he asked.

100

'No, she went peacefully by the looks of it. We found this wrapped around her hand, though, must've been special.'

Maguire took the medallion and studied it closely. One side bore the likeness of a man's profile, the other was engraved with the words 'Saint Jerome'.

'God rest her soul,' he said. 'Lord knows she deserves it.'

The medic pulled a sheet over her face.

'Would you happen to know,' he asked, 'if she has any next of kin?'

Maguire hesitated, took the envelope from O'Brien and handed it to the medic.

'As a matter of fact, she does,' he said. 'She's a son, at Saint Jerome's. His name is Brennan. Father Patrick Brennan.'

The End

THE GIRL FROM KILKENNY

Sample chapter

Nancy had much to be grateful for, not least her husband, for it was Fearghus McBride who'd given her a sense of purpose, a direction in life. It was Fearghus who'd loved her for who she was, despite the mood swings and inexplicable silences that would last for days. It was Fearghus who'd taught her how to smile. It was Fearghus who'd given her hope for the future. As she gazed out across the lush, green field where the sheep used to graze and the lambs used to bleat, she realised he'd given her something else, too. Something she hadn't counted on. Despair.

She toyed with the ring on her finger. Eighteen carats of white gold. Diamond inlay. It had a value, but no longer the sentimental kind, a few hundred, maybe, perhaps a grand. Enough to tide her over for a couple of months. She could sell it, but not in Kinsale, not even Cork.

Eyebrows would be raised, questions would be asked, rumours would start to spread. She'd have to go elsewhere, somewhere farther afield, somewhere where she wouldn't be recognised. If only Fearghus had kept up the premiums on the livestock insurance she wouldn't have to stoop to selling her jewellery. If only he'd put in a claim for compensation for the loss of the sheep, then perhaps they wouldn't be living hand to mouth. If only he'd faced up to his responsibilities. If only.

* * *

'Sorry,' she whispered, as she stroked his head and returned to the task at hand, 'I'm so sorry.' She cleared her throat, picked up the cleaver and brought it down hard. It slammed through his leg, severing it just above the knee. There was no blood to speak of, just a sad, sorry look of betrayal in his big, innocent eyes. She rolled him onto his back, hesitated as she crossed herself then brought the cleaver down for a final time, grimacing as his head parted company with the body. She wiped her dry, cracked lips with the back of her hand and, holding him gently across the belly, picked up the paring knife. The blade sliced silently through his skin as she drew the knife the length of his torso. Close to tears in the fading light, she slipped her fingers beneath the wound and, to the sound of a silk sheet being slowly torn in two, gently teased the skin from the flesh.

She froze as the front door slammed, cocked her head and listened. Muffled footsteps shuffled down the hall. She drew a breath, a long, deep breath and held it. The veins in her arm bulged as she gripped the knife. The kitchen door creaked open. Fearghus, silhouetted by the light from the hall, stood and scowled in disgust.

'Rabbit?' he barked. 'For feck's sake, Nancy, can we not eat something else?'

Nancy sighed, traced an index finger along the buck's naked stomach and sliced it open before reaching in and yanking the intestines free. A single tear clung to her eye.

'It's all we have,' she sniffed. 'Just be grateful. This fella gave his life for you, just so's you can fill your belly.'

'What?'

'One minute he's bounding round the field, happy as Larry, not a care in the world, next thing, he's in the feckin' snare. It's not right.'

'But…'

'Can you not at least shoot them, or borrow a ferret? Winding up dead with a length of wire round your neck is no way to go, it's too feckin' painful. Tis torture, so it is.'

Fearghus kept his distance. There were times, he'd learned from experience, when it was wiser to say little and do nothing.

'Are you okay?' he asked softly.

Nancy paused, opened her mouth as if to speak, then thought the better of it. The last thing she wanted was another argument, another fight, another spat over something that was out of their hands.

'You're filthy,' she said, forcing a smile. 'You've mud everywhere. Why don't you take yourself off and have a shower? There's plenty of water, so.'

'In a bit,' said Fearghus, 'I want to look at the paperwork first.'

Nancy clenched her teeth and swallowed hard, forcing back the months of frustration which threatened to spew at the slightest provocation. It was obvious that remaining in the same room, breathing the same air and sharing the same meal with the man she'd married was becoming increasingly difficult. She was suffocating.

'Christ, I need a drink,' she mumbled to herself.

'What's that?'

'A drink,' she yelled, 'I need a feckin' drink!'

Fearghus, accustomed as he was to what he described as 'irrational and unfounded hormonal outbursts', smiled gently and beckoned his wife to the table.

'Come so,' he said, setting down a clay bottle, 'it's your lucky day. Poteen, from me Da, he'll be along soon.'

Nancy took two tumblers from the wall cabinet, sat down and filled the glasses with a generous dose of the toxic potato juice as Fearghus randomly waded through a mound of papers, bills and final demands.

'So, how's it looking?' asked Nancy, coughing as the whiskey burned her throat.

'Well,' said Fearghus, 'looks like we're down to our last million. We'll have to let the servants go.'

'Be serious.'

'Not great. We still owe for the feed and the concentrates even though we've no sheep left. And the oil's gone up, just like everything else.'

'Do we need the oil?' asked Nancy, as if she cared.

'Sure, no, not really. We'll just freeze to death when the bastard cold sets in.'

'Not a bad idea,' she said, gazing at the ceiling, her thoughts wandering. 'Maybe we should change, start anew, go dairy. Maybe.'

'Now, that's a grand idea,' said Fearghus. 'All we have to do is build a milking parlour, get some cattle and wait for the supermarkets to pay us a penny a pint for our trouble.'

'Just a suggestion. I could milk them. That would save on the cost.'

'You, with a fistful of udders. Are you mad?'

'Pity. Quite fancied one of those milkmaid outfits.'

Fearghus grinned. As usual, the storm clouds were passing and Nancy was softening, helped in no small way by the poteen. She downed her glass, wheezed, and filled it up again.

'Okay. Let's forget the livestock,' she said. 'Why not crop the whole lot?'

'And what do you suggest we plant? Mangoes? Cotton, maybe?'

'Kestrel. They're hardy enough, and…'

'Spuds? That's what got this country into trouble in the first place.'

'Well, we can't use the field for grazing anymore, not till we get the all clear. We can't go on like this, Fearghus, we have to do something or I'll end up feckin' killing you. So help me, I'll…'

Nancy jumped as the door flew open.

'Now, now, what's all this, then?' said Brendan. 'I can hear you two down the hall.'

'Brendan, didn't hear you come in,' said Nancy.

'Not surprised.'

'Hello, Da,' said Fearghus. 'Still raining?'

'A few spots, nothing to worry about,' said Brendan. 'Now, I'll take a glass of that, if you don't mind,' he said, nodding towards the poteen.

Nancy managed a smile for her father-in-law as he slumped in the armchair, his boots caked in mud, his jacket drenched. Raindrops gathered on the peak of his cap and fell, one by one, to his lap.

'Sure, I don't know what you see in it,' said Nancy as she passed him a glass of whiskey. 'All that walking, day in, day out.'

'You should try it, lass. Come a walk with me next time. All that clean air, good for the soul, so it is.'

'Good, my arse,' she said. 'Where'd you go?'

'The river,' said Brendan. 'Over by Whitecastle.'

'Whitecastle?' said Fearghus. 'But that's feckin' miles away.'

'I know. But it's where I have to go.'

'Still looking for those coins, Brendan?' asked Nancy.

'I am. And I've two more, now.'

'So, how many's that, in total?'

'Six, I think.'

Nancy shook her head and sighed with a puff of the cheeks. Fearghus and Brendan watched in silence as she returned to the sink, jointed the rabbit and tossed it into a casserole. Fearghus caught her eye. Her vacant gaze troubled him.

'I'm away, so,' she said, wiping her hands on her jumper.

'What?' said Fearghus. 'In this weather? Where will you be going at this time...'

'Out. Just out.'

'Why?' said Fearghus. 'Will you not just sit with us and...'

'No. I can't listen to you talking about the farm anymore, Fearghus. I can't take it. It's our livelihood and all you do is talk, talk, talk. Just do something about it. Stop talking and feckin' do something.'

'Ah, come on, Nancy, there's no need for...'

'Let her go,' said Brendan as the door closed behind her. 'Let her go. You may have been married nine years, son, but you've still a lot to learn. She'll be fine, soon enough, she'll be fine.'

* * *

Nancy knew the lane like the back of her hand. So well in fact, she could walk it blindfolded. With the low cloud, no moonlight, and a fine, persistent drizzle, she may as well have been. She had no intention of going to town. There was nowhere in particular she wanted to visit, no-one she wanted to see, her feet simply led her there.

Forty minutes later she arrived in Market Square, stood for a moment and shivered, as though she was surprised to be there. The only sign of life came from The Grey Hound. With its misted windows and soft, yellow light, it looked warm and inviting. She drove her hands into her pockets and fumbled for any loose change. She could tell, simply by the feel of the coins, that she had enough, just enough, for a half pint of Murphy's.

'Nancy!' said Aiden. 'Looking lovely as ever!'

Embarrassed, Nancy coyly tucked a tress of sodden, raven black hair behind her ear and smiled.

'Stop now,' she said softly.

'If it's Fearghus you're after, I've not seen him.'

'No, I was just, I just fancied…'

She paused and locked eyes with a stranger seated at the bar. He was young, at least ten years younger than herself. Dressed in an Argyll sweater, beige chinos and college loafers, he looked as though he'd stepped from the pages of a vintage clothing catalogue. '*Another feckin' tourist*,' she thought. He grinned to reveal a set of cosmetically enhanced teeth and raised his glass.

'He's right you know, you do look lovely,' he said, with a predatory glint in his eye.

The accent grated on her. It could have been West Coast, it could have been the Deep South or even New York, she didn't know and she didn't care. It was American and that was enough to raise her hackles.

'Don't tell me,' she said with disdain, 'your great, great, grandfather was called Seamus O'Flaherty, he was born in Kinsale to a family of leprechauns, and you've come to find his grave.'

The stranger smirked, took a sip of whiskey, and slowly set his glass atop the bar.

'Actually, he was called Antonio Balducci, he was born in Naples, lived on the Via Nardones, and he's buried in the Cimitero di Poggioreale.'

'Oh.'

'I'm here for the golf. My pals are out back, in the snug.'

Aiden glanced at Nancy and winked.

'Drink?' asked the stranger, 'what'll you have?'

Nancy hesitated, shuffled nervously from foot to foot and turned for the door.

'No, I'd best be off,' she said.

'Aw, come on,' he said as he pulled a wallet from his back pocket. 'Have one on me. No hard feelings, huh? I'm Josh, Josh Balducci. One hundred percent Italian-American. Not an ounce of Irish, guaranteed.'

Nancy caught sight of the stranger's wallet. She had never seen so many banknotes crammed together in such a small place before. So many banknotes with a '50' printed in the top right hand corner. She blinked, rapidly, as though afflicted by a tic and nibbled the nail on her right index finger.

'Paddy's,' she mumbled, keeping her distance. 'Paddy's, a large one. Thanks.'

'Well,' said Josh. 'I know your name's Nancy, and you don't look like a golfer, so I assume you live here, right?'

Nancy glared at him contemptuously.

'Christ, you're clever,' she said. 'You should be a detective.'

'Too dangerous. I like to play safe. Accountants are safe.'

'Sláinte,' she said, knocking back the whiskey. 'I have to go.'

'So soon? But we've only just met, have another, I promise I won't bite.'

'Sorry.'

'Tomorrow, then?'

She hesitated.

'No, No,' she said. 'Maybe.'

Flustered, she bowed her head and left.

Want to read on? The Girl from Kilkenny is available on Kindle and in paperback from Amazon.

If you enjoyed this book, please let others know by leaving a quick review on Amazon. Also, if you spot anything untoward in the paperback, get in touch. We strive for the best quality and appreciate reader feedback.

editor@thebookfolks.com

www.thebookfolks.com

Manufactured by Amazon.ca
Bolton, ON